DATE DUE

Zeeland,
or
Elective Concurrences

ALSO BY HANS KONING

(WRITING UNTIL 1972 UNDER THE NAME HANS KONINGSBERGER)

(FICTION)

The Affair

An American Romance

A Walk with Love and Death

I Know What I'm Doing

The Revolutionary

Death of a Schoolboy

The Petersburg-Cannes Express

The Kleber Flight

DeWitt's War

America Made Me

Acts of Faith

Pursuit of a Woman on the Hinge of History

(NONFICTION)

Love and Hate in China

Along the Roads of Russia

The Future of Che Guevara

The Almost World

The World of Vermeer

A New Yorker in Egypt

Nineteen Sixty-Eight

Columbus: His Enterprise

The Conquest of America

Zeeland, *or* Elective Concurrences

A Novel

HANS KONING

NewSouth Books
Montgomery

NewSouth Books
P.O. Box 1588
Montgomery, AL 36102

This book is a work of fiction. Names, characters, places, and incidents are either products of the author's imagination or are used fictitiously. Any resemblance to actual events or locales or persons, living or dead, is entirely coincidental.

 Published in the United States by NewSouth Books, a division of NewSouth, Inc., Montgomery, Alabama.

Library of Congress Cataloging-in-Publication Data
Koning, Hans.
Zeeland, or, Elective concurrences : a novel / by Hans Koning
p. cm.
ISBN 1-58838-050-5
1. France—History—German occupation, 1949–1945—Fiction.
2. World War, 1939–1945—France—Fiction.
3. Americans—France—Fiction. 4. Americans—Fiction.
5. Grandfathers—Fiction. 6. Soldiers—Fiction.
I. Title: Zeeland. II. Title: Elective concurrences. III. Title.
PS3561.046 Z44 2001
813'.54--dc21
2001055722

Book Design by Randall Williams
Printed in the United States of America
by Phoenix Color Corporation

First Edition

A Preamble

THIS STORY DESCRIBES TWO TURNING POINTS OF WAR IN a family chronicle. It is told, of course, in the manner people spoke and thought at the time.

In certain ways life was darker then, but it also was less *random.* There was more certainty about human destiny, which seemed fated to go *per ardua ad astra,* through the thorns to the stars, as they said in the RAF.

I believe in free will but also in the logic of history. We no longer deal in "elective affinities," emotions inherent in the material world, nature "abhorring" a vacuum, that kind of thing. Goethe was into that. But the logic of history has given us the "elective concurrences" of the title instead.

"They help us, as they create a sense of order in the human chaos," as ex-sergeant Michael Beauchamp once said in a letter.

Michael, in 1941

I

A decrepit Belgian train is making its way from Brussels to Charleroi near the French border. The third-class compartment is packed. Its window has been opened through the combined efforts of several passengers but the train goes too slow to create any breeze. Flies are circling around people's faces.

It is silent in the compartment and everyone is staring into space. That is because the year is 1941. There is a war on, Belgium is occupied by the Germans. If they win, Belgium together with Holland will be put in the "Westmark," part of Germany. But that outcome is now in doubt.

A tall and very thin young man sits squeezed in a corner, his head leaning back against the wooden partition. His eyes are closed but he's only pretending to be asleep: a careful observer would notice the alertness in his arms and hands. His name is Michael Beauchamp and he is an American, but on the Belgian identity card in the inside pocket of his ill-fitting jacket it says Guillaume Roux, Belgian apprentice miner, resident of the town of Huy.

A heavy German noncom, apparently not armed except for the standard dagger in his belt, his uniform jacket only reaching halfway down his behind, a metal breastplate hanging from a long chain around his neck, works his way through the mass of travelers standing or sitting on their suitcases in the corridor. He is inspecting everyone's papers. When he takes his position in the doorway of the compartment and says in German and French, "Ausweise—papiers," Michael opens his eyes and sees before them the metal breastplate which, he thinks, gives the German something of the effect of a medieval warrior. But then he raises his head and sees the soldier's face, sees it's the face of a farmer, with the quiet, dull, look of a countryman without curiosity.

Michael hands him his miner's identification. Under the little photograph of Michael, the picture of the real owner is still glued on; presumably the man who fixed the document for him thought he'd ruin the card if he tried to pry it off. The two pictures make a precise fit, the original one doesn't stick out, but it makes the photograph of Michael thicker than it should be. Michael is aware of this imperfection but he keeps quite calm while the soldier looks at the picture and from the picture back to him. Michael concentrates on the breastplate which has a word in heraldic writing engraved on it. When he has made out that it says, "Feldgendarmerie," he already has his card handed back to him.

The departure of the German changes the mood in the compartment. When they hear him call for "Ausweise" in the next compartment, some of the passengers smile at each other. Now conversations start, in French and in Flemish, about food mostly and rationing. Michael wonders if that sense of relief in the air means that there are others also traveling with false papers.

He studies the faces. None of them look like that, but you

can't tell. Four men—that one must be a civil servant, his neighbor a minor railroad functionary, no, such a man would have got himself a more comfortable seat on this train, a post office worker then, next a carpenter or a mason or someone like that, big hands, biceps, then opposite him a retired schoolteacher who's kept his hat on in spite of the heat. Two women—two big women, sisters possibly, must be Bruxelloises, going into the countryside to scrounge up black market food.

He thinks back to riding the subway in New York, the almost immeasurable difference, a world that is centuries away from this one where the alertness of a German noncom would have condemned him to a hasty death.

When the train reaches Charleroi, it is getting dark. Michael waits in order to be the last one off, and when he stands on the platform it lies empty before him. There is no policeman at the exit, only a railroad worker who sits on a bench, smoking. He looks up at Michael and says, "You'd better hurry, son, curfew soon." That's what Michael understands him to say: his French is adequate, and then "couvre-feu" is clearly the same as "curfew."

The little station square is empty, too. The houses have their blackout curtains drawn, only at one does he see a crack of yellow light. In the middle of the square stand a couple of trees, and there's a dry fountain with a stone seat. When they gave him his fake miner's card in Brussels, he was told there'd be someone meeting this train, someone who'd help him across the French border and on to the next contact person. But nothing stirs. He crosses over to the fountain and sits down on the seat which is still warm from the sun.

Michael has been on the road for four days and he feels himself dozing off, he almost slid off the bench. He jumps up and starts pacing. Three avenues radiate out from the square, none showing any life. Only behind the glass of the station entrance a lamp, painted over, sends out some dark-blue light. He tries the door but it is locked. I'm the last fucking man on earth. Not a sound. He shivers.

He sees two slits of light approach from far off on one of the avenues, a car's headlights which have been pasted over with just a narrow opening left. He presses himself in the corner beside the door and turns his head to the wall; in the dark a face is the most visible part of a person. He hears the car make the round of the fountain, it does not stop and vanishes down the next avenue. Michael starts to walk down the avenue from which the car emerged, going close to the wall, as fast as he can. Every now and again he pauses and listens.

He passes a door and hears voices behind it. There is a hint of light behind the transom. He knocks on the door. Sudden silence. He knocks once more and sees that the glimmer of light has been extinguished. He goes on, he passes a shop window. It's empty of whatever goods they may once have sold but there is a movement in the back, a door being closed. He knocks on the window with a coin. He is about to give up when he hears the street door beyond the window open. It is on a chain and there is someone standing behind it, he cannot make out if it's a man or a woman. He waits, but the person does not speak.

"I'm an escaped prisoner of war," he says in a low voice, in French. "I'm stuck in the curfew. Will you help me?"

A pause. "Do you have matches?" It's a woman's voice.

"Eh? Yes."

"Light one. I want to see your face."

Michael obeys and holds the lighted match beside his head.

Michael, 1941

The woman closes the door. "Wait, wait," he says, for he has noticed the sound of a car approaching. But the woman had closed the door to take off the chain, and she now lets him in.

Michael, in 1941

2

Michael Beauchamp had been very lucky. The house in Charleroi where they let him in belongs to a man the town calls Dr. Tiche, no one remembers why, because he is not a doctor, he is an antique dealer. Madame Tiche is the woman who opened the door for Michael. They're people who have traveled much and who speak English. They're not parochial. They seat Michael at the kitchen table and give him a cup of chicory coffee.

"You are an escaped prisoner of war?" Dr. Tiche asks. "You're not a Frenchman, there's an accent."

"I'm an American."

They stare at him.

"I was a student at Sheffield University when the war broke out. And then I enlisted with the Brits. I'm not sure why," he adds with a little laugh. "Anyway, I'm in the Commandos."

Tiche and wife look at each other. "You must forgive us if we are surprised," Dr. Tiche says, now switching to English. "An American prisoner of war? And what are the Commandos?"

"Did you hear about the raid on St. Nazaire?" Michael asks. "The first one? I was in on that. Some Canadians too. We couldn't get back to our boat and the Germans caught us and sent us to a prison camp. For me Stalag Seven, near Stuttgart."

It is early in the war. Later, Dr. Tiche and his wife will become more careful and suspicious (to no avail, though, for they will both end up in Mauthausen concentration camp). But we are now in June 1941. England has gone through the threat of invasion and the London blitz, and Russia is about to be attacked by the Germans. The United States is still officially neutral.

"Well," Madame Tiche says, "You surely got a long way from Stuttgart already. Not that I know where that is exactly."

"There are lines," Michael tells them, "organized lines of people who help us. Like the underground railroad to Canada once for escaped slaves from the U.S., you know? But something has gone wrong. They say that Heydrich is in Paris, he is the big boss in the SS, and that there have been mass arrests. My contact in this town didn't show up at the station tonight."

"What was his name?" Dr. Tiche asks, "Or her name?"

Michael frowns. "We don't get to know names."

"Of course he can't tell us that," Madame Tiche says. "Let's call you John. John, are you hungry? We can give you a sandwich. We don't have any butter left but we do have something jokingly called paté."

"I'll be out of here tomorrow morning, as soon as the curfew lifts, six o'clock," Michael answers. "But yes, I would love a sandwich."

"And once you're out of here?" Dr. Tiche asks.

"I'll manage. I just have to get to Vichy. We still have some kind of consulate there, a liaison office with the Pétain government, as far as I could find out in the camp."

Dr. Tiche looks at him. He hesitates. Then he says, "The French border is no problem here, Belgium and the north of

France are one German military district. But to get to Vichy, you have to cross the border of the Zone. To the unoccupied zone. That's very tough without the official permits."

"I know," Michael says, "I've looked at the map. I think I can swim that river. The Cher it's called."

"I think you underestimate—" Tiche begins.

"Of course, we—" says his wife.

They begin to laugh. "I have friends," Tiche says. "We'll help you."

Michael looks embarrassed. "I've always been told—"

"Tell me," Tiche interrupts. "Who is the American Secretary of War?"

Michael reddens. "I—I don't remember."

"Tiche," Madame says, "I think—"

"Stimson," Michael cries. "Henry Stimson."

"And who—"

"Stop this, Tiche. Right now."

TWO DAYS LATER Michael is on a train again, for Vichy, with a brand-new, genuine, zone traffic *Ausweis* in his pocket. His name this time is Joseph Auteuil, medical student, resident of Montrichard, a little town on the Cher river. He has to change at Vierzon where the German control posts are. It all goes smoothly.

Seven in the morning: Michael arrives at Vichy-Gare. The train is six hours late and he is slightly the worse for wear, but there are no German uniforms in sight here and he feels a new charge of optimism and energy. He enters the first café he comes to outside the station and has a chicory coffee. They don't have croissants but they give him two slices of dark bread. On the bar stool next to him, a bearded man is looking through various books he has put on the counter, and when their eyes meet, Michael asks him how to get to the university.

He has an idea that he could use his medical student identity card to cadge some cheap meals and even lodging, maybe.

The bearded man focuses on him and frowns nervously. "There is no university in Vichy," he informs Michael and dives back into his books. A waiter who has monitored their exchange takes this as his key to present Michael with the tab. "Ten francs?" Michael asks, too loudly.

The waiter eyes him in silence; Michael puts the money on the counter and gets out of there. A neat old gentleman sitting on a bench with a newspaper tells him that the American legation is housed in the Villa Ica but he declares himself unable to explain the way there. Michael asks various passers-by until a woman in a bookstore explains to him where it is, adding that he should take a taxi (a horse-taxi, that is) because it is too far to walk. But after his disastrous breakfast he has only seventeen francs left and he walks, twice getting lost. It's several hours later when he stands at the gate of a remarkably ugly building mixing the styles of all continents.

A French policeman is guarding the entrance but he is busy cleaning his nails and shows no interest in Michael who rings the bell. A sign next to it announces in two languages, "Hours ten to twelve, Monday, Wednesday, Friday." Michael tries to list the happenings of the past week to find what day it is but doesn't succeed. He feels exhausted and is tempted to go away but doesn't. I won't get far with seventeen francs, he thinks. Maybe they know of a room for me, maybe they'll let me take a shower. The consul will invite me to dinner and we'll talk over our scotches, and he'll end up finding an old suit for me to wear. You're doing your bit for all of us, he'll say when Michael tells him he can't accept it—

The door opens and he sees a middle-aged woman, very American looking with a gray perm. She steps aside and lets him enter the little office which sits right behind the door. It only holds a desk and two chairs.

Michael introduces himself.

The woman looks surprised at this compatriot of hers who is unshaven, wears a suit which is much too tight, and looks as if he had slept in it for a week (he has), and who now appears in the middle of France.

"I would like to see the attaché or whatever he is called," Michael says and then sees that was a bad start. "Whatever he is called indeed," she repeats indignantly.

"I meant—"

"May I see your passport?" She has a Southern accent.

"I don't have it. I am an escaped prisoner of war from Germany."

She does not seem startled by this. In fact, he thinks, she hasn't listened. "Do you have *any* kind of identification?" she asks.

Better not show the *Ausweis*, he thinks. False papers are bound to make her nervous. "No," he says, "but I do exist," this with a smile to show her his pleasant temper. "I have people in the U.S. you could phone."

"What precisely do you want of us?" she asks.

"Your help to get out of the country."

"To return to the States."

"Well, yes. To England, that is."

A silence.

"Did I hear you say you are an escaped prisoner of war?" So

she has heard but clearly hopes she had heard wrong.

"That's what I said!"

"Don't yell at me, young man."

"I'm not yelling, ma'am. Yelling implies a high-pitched voice. I'm much too tired to yell. Can I see the attaché?"

"No one in this mission can be seen without previous appointment. You may write to us and explain your purpose. You will then be contacted, also *by mail.*"

Michael produces a bitter little laugh. "That will be difficult. I have no address. For your information. I have no address, no money, no, wait"—he puts his hand in his pocket and brings out a fistful of coins—"I have seventeen francs. I have no passport. I'm still an American citizen and as such with the right to see the attaché."

"I myself can tell you that you missed the boat, young man. Last month, on May 15 to be precise, Germany stopped giving exit visas to American citizens."

Well, you certainly look as if you enjoyed telling me that, you old bastard, Michael says, but only to himself.

"You were made a prisoner in a battle with German forces?" she then asks.

"Yes."

"And at the time you were a member of the armed forces of another nation?"

No, I was a dwarf representing Santa Claus. "Yes," he says, too loud again. "Of the British army."

She takes a deep breath. "Are you aware of the law which deprives a United States citizen serving in a foreign army of his citizenship? Which means that after you— Wait! What are you doing?"

Michael has jumped up, and going around her desk, opens

the door behind her. He looks into an empty office. The curtains are drawn and it is almost dark in there.

The woman pulls the doorknob out of his hands and slams the door shut. "I don't like to call the French policeman in here," she announces, "but if you don't leave, I will do just that."

Michael walks out. "Remember," she calls after him, "One always writes first."

"Yes, and fuck you too," Michael says before slamming the door.

He stands outside and thinks, I surely handled that very nicely. Just the right mix of charm and military directness. What an ass I am.

He looks at the little villas across the street and back at Villa Ica. They all stand there on parade, those houses, immobile, staring at him with complacency. If you'd only conform, they say, one carries one's passport and one writes first. They are thoroughly satisfied with the moral lesson he has received by having been thrown out.

He turns the other corner and walks on without knowing where to go next. Suddenly he comes upon a decrepit little sign. "Chez Jo," it says. Below it some steps lead to a shuttered window.

Jo belongs here as little as I do, he thinks. He goes down the steps and finds a half-dark barroom. He orders a glass of white wine after studying the price list on the wall. "No, red, s'il vous plaît." Red is thirty centimes cheaper.

Michel, in 1871

3

Michael is an American. His grandfather Michel Beauchamp was French and became the first Beauchamp to be caught up in a German war. This is what happened to him.

Michel Beauchamp was a printer, a young married man living in Paris when the French-German war broke out in the summer of 1870. His parents had sent him to the Collége Chaptal to study the classics, they had great plans for him but they ran out of money. The boy was offered a grant to study for the priesthood but he refused; his Latin got him a job as an apprentice in the famous Descartes Printing Works. Three years later he was independent and had established himself as an excellent craftsman. The logo of the Imprimerie Beauchamp, a tree in a meadow (Beau champ: fair field) was already well known.

By winter 1870, Paris was cut off and under German siege. In March 1871 the beleaguered Parisians created a commune to run their city and to continue the war which the French government, now in Versailles, had given up on at the end of January when they signed an armistice. Michel Beauchamp believed in the Commune and printed many of its proclamations.

In the last days of May the soldiers of the French government retook the capital street by street. The government showed a fierce determination they had unfortunately lacked when fighting the Prussians. The Commune was labeled traitorous. It had a hundred thousand National Guardsmen under arms, but most of these were untrained. They fought a guerrilla war of defense, burned down government buildings, and shot hostages. After their collapse, the Versailles government put thousands of Commune supporters and suspected supporters under arrest.

Every man or woman who had stains on their hands from gunpowder or perhaps it was from soot or ink, or who had joined a workmen's union or was denounced by a neighbor, was shot—more than twenty thousand of them. The others were deported to Devil's Island or to Algeria, or locked up in prisons and army fortresses.

Later this was called "the week of blood," but the mutual hatred between the citizens of the same country lasted, perhaps, though hidden, to our present day. Half the plumbers, roofers, shoemakers, house painters, and so forth, of Paris had been executed. As for Michel, he was arrested one morning at his printing works and after a two-minute trial (confrontation would be the better word) condemned to death.

His wife Anne, four months pregnant, set out on a round of police barracks and prisons to find her vanished husband. The city had become unrecognizable to her with its empty streets soundless under the May sunshine, buildings burned out and still smoking and smouldering, the barricades of wrecked furniture and paving stones still blocking crossroads, a smell of blood, real or imagined, permeating the air, and then suddenly across an invisible barrier, packed café terraces, ladies in long dresses strolling along an avenue with gentlemen in gloves and spats.

On her third day a clerk took pity on her desperate appearance and sent her to the Bons Enfants barracks where, he had heard, they were trying to make lists of the more prominent arrests and executions. Anne waited there half a day until a police officer came out and gave her an iron ring with a little star soldered onto it, which she recognized as her husband's. "The Communard Michel Beauchamp has been executed," the policeman said.

She stood outside the gate, clutching the ring. She went up to a tree across the road. It was a late spring; its leaves were still small and of a beautiful soft green, shining with rain drops. She leaned her face against the bark and embraced the tree. She did not cry.

She did not go back home but kept going. She fled to Le Havre, the town of her childhood, walking all the way. When she saw men in the distance, French soldiers in uniform, or deserters, or men just lost, or when the spiked helmets of a patrol of Prussian Uhlanen came into view, she ran out into the fields and hid. She carried money: when she set out on her search, she had taken their savings, almost a thousand francs in coin, with her. She had hoped it might be possible to bribe prison guards into releasing Michel.

After a month in Le Havre she bought passage on a paddle-steamer bound for Philadelphia, and thus, in November 1871, the son of Michel and Anne Beauchamp came to be born in the United States from a mother who taught him a vague hatred of France. She named him Michel after his father, and she never remarried.

Her son married late in life only, when "Michel" had become "Michael" and the family, still in Philadelphia, had dropped a pronunciation of their name as "Beechum" and gone back to the original pronunciation "Bochan," possibly on a wave of pro-Allied feelings during the first World War. And the son of that Michel-later-Michael, also called Michael, was born in 1921, when his father was forty-nine. He was the young man hiding from the curfew patrol in Charleroi in 1941, and saying "fuck you" to a Nashville lady working at the American legation in Vichy.

THE POLICE CORPORAL who informed Anne Beauchamp that her husband had been shot was mistaken. For unknown reasons Beauchamp had been left behind as his cellmates were taken out each day to be lined up against the wall in an abandoned cloister garden and executed. Finally, at dawn on June 5, 1871, a foggy, drizzly morning, he was among the remaining men who were marched down the Route Nationale for Auxerre, with some mounted soldiers guarding them. They were on their way to Bordeaux, marked for deportation to Algeria. A whim of fate or of a weary or indifferent officer, had put him among them.

The choice between life and death for a Paris Commune printer, in June 1871, cannot seem crucial so many years—three generations—later. We have enough political outrages, and to spare, of our own to focus on.

And beyond that, how would it matter that the printer Beauchamp did not get shot in 1871, but came to his end ten or fifteen years later on the quayside of a North African harbor that looked out over the Mediterranean glittering in the morning sun? Is there still a Michel-Beauchamp consciousness alive in the universe, able to feel regret or non-regret? He himself certainly did not believe there would be after his death.

Yet the life of one human being may bear on other lives in a myriad ways, through time. Such acting-upon may simply lie within the logic of human connections. But rarely it may appear so fated that it is almost unavoidable to describe it as an act of will. People who have religion will speak of the will of God. Others who are agnostics (as Beauchamp probably was) or who just don't believe in talking of God if it seems the easy but not necessary "way out," may accept that an intense emotion or act of will could cling to a place beyond the life of its originator and then steer others. They wouldn't be able to explain it in Newtonian terms but it would be as little "supernatural" as gravity is supernatural. It is metaphysics and one day it may be physics.

And to the degree that a sequel or concurrence of events would thus appear to have been *willed*, it can be called elective, that is, chosen rather than fortuitous and coincidental. "Elective" was the term coined by a Swedish eighteenth century chemist for certain chemical interactions; it was Goethe who then, rather dubiously, transferred this concept of "near free-will" from chemical substances to human affection and disaffection. "Elective" may go from the (seemingly) free will of atoms to our (almost) free will in the world of coincidence—and beyond that. Or so one may choose to believe.

THE DEPORTEES had been marched along the Nationale (as they called it) for three days. Nights they were locked up in stables or army storage rooms. Guards were posted, there were no escapes.

On the fourth day, which began in a dense fog, the sun

came out and it suddenly grew hot in the humid air. That morning there had been nothing to eat or drink for them, and when they came to a river bridge, the sergeant in charge decided to let them drink from the stream. They were halted at the foot of the bridge: the river ran between brick walls there and after all the rainstorms of that spring the water had risen to within a foot of the top.

The men lay down on their stomachs and bending their heads down, slurped the dirty, foam-covered, water. The soldiers had their own flasks of wine and water, but they let their horses drink from the river.

And so little have some of us learned to expect of life, that among these deportees (condemned without trial, dragged away from wives and children and friends) there were men who thought, "That sarge isn't such a bad chap"—because he could just as well have had them march on, parched or not, along the bridge.

A shout was heard. Some of the men got to their feet and pointed: a prisoner was in the water and the current carried him away. The nearest soldier looked at his sergeant to see what he was to do. "Shoot him!" the sergeant cried.

The soldier hesitated for he thought that the prisoner had fallen in, but then he pulled his horse-pistol which he was carrying cocked, let it rest on his left arm, aimed, and pulled the trigger. The prisoner was just then floating past him, prone, his face under water. The shot went off, the man in the water raised his head, uttered a cry, and went under.

"Fall in, form ranks! On your feet!" the sergeant shouted, galloping along the shoreline within inches of the men. When he saw them obey, he rode out on the bridge and stared upstream and downstream. "I think you got him," he went to tell the soldier who had fired. "That's a fine pistol you have there. Can I see it?"

The soldier nodded and pointed to a reddish stain on the water, still visible but rapidly being dispersed. "Got him," he said.

Those were the final words spoken about the vanished prisoner.

Michel Beauchamp was washed ashore a mile down river from the bridge. The water carried him onto a small ridge of earth sticking out over the surface. It looked as if it had broken off from the cliff above it. Michel crawled toward the trees, but he could not manage the climb. He lost consciousness.

When he came to, it was raining. The side of his head hurt blindingly and when he touched it, he felt a sticky crust of coagulated blood. The river water had begun covering his ridge; he washed his head and face as well as he could and drank. Then he climbed up to where the trees grew and started walking away from the river. He was dizzy and shivering in the warm air, holding on to one tree after another. He remembered the sound of the pistol shot but did not know if a bullet had hit him or if perhaps it had been a rock in the river. He could feel that his wound had started bleeding again but he kept going. It was as if the trees were passing him on from one to another, oak trees giving out some of their strength to him. He felt as if the trees had arms, as in the fairy tale book he had owned as a child. He saw the arms. How kind these trees are, if only they grew closer together, he thought. Sometimes the gap was so large, they almost dropped him in the middle.

But then he came to where the trees ended, and he could see the sky. It was darkening already, with ragged rain clouds chasing across. In the distance stood a farm building and some kind of storage shed was not more than a hundred feet away from him.

"I'll make it," he said, and he did. He found it was filled with bales of hay. He waited and watched, but he heard nothing, neither man nor animal. He crawled between two bales, covered himself with loose hay as well as he could. He slept.

Michel, in 1871

4

Oak trees. Oak trees. The words kept vibrating in his head and ended up waking him. He lay very still for his head felt like an egg shell. Tiliae contermina quercus. A Latin poem about trees? No, there was more to it, but he couldn't remember. In school they had been told the story about a poet exiled from Athens: shivering and half-naked in the market place of a foreign town, he climbed on a rock and started quoting Homer, verses about Odysseus washed ashore on Skeria, and the people stopped to listen and offered him food and shelter. Shall I go to the nearest town and start citing Victor Hugo? "And if there's but one left, I will be that one"—and then will they feed me?

The war is over and the Commune is over and done with. He thought of an evening, listening with Anne to their friends talking of the new community they would create. "Those long words that have the power to make us so unhappy," she had said afterward. Had it all been a terrifying mistake? But still, hadn't there been moments through it all of more hope and excitement, exultation wasn't too strong a word, than ever, anywhere, in the world? How else would people begin again with the Year One? Those young men in their white foulards, as if already touched by the guillotine— He sat upright, put his hand to his wound. It felt dry. Get going, get away from that river.

He was still wearing the clothes he had come to work in that morning when two police officers had been waiting for him in his office, except for the jacket and hat which were gone, and so were his watch and his ring. His shoes were cracked from the river water. I have no papers, there is the rub. Everyone will be my enemy, I have to steer south, away from Paris and the armies. But I have to get a message to Anne, fast, or she may believe me dead. The bureaucrats. They mislaid my death. Am I grateful to be alive? Yes, but only because of Anne.

Then he felt a stronger fear invade him than he had experienced the nights in the Bons Enfants barracks waiting for the dawn deaths list. He felt the bullets biting through his skin. How dare they, he thought. How dare any man commit this outrage on another, destroy a body like his own.

He went to stand in the door opening of the shed and looked out. It was raining softly. He was pleased; in the rain you are less obvious. The outline of the farm was now barely visible. He took a step outside and tilted his head to the rain, he felt stronger than he had expected.

He went back into the wood and then circled the farm, and continued away from the river in what he hoped was a southernly direction. There was plenty of water to drink, too much, ponds and puddles everywhere, but nothing that would serve as food. Later the ground started to rise and the earth, covered with some kind of heather, was dry. He lay down for a rest but the insects started attacking him and he gave up and went on.

The rise ended at a ridge and in front of him the ground sloped down to a valley, and at its bottom ran a narrow railroad. There was no sign of a human presence. He climbed down and started walking between the rails.

When he came to a pile of crossbeams stacked beside the track, he pulled one out and several more came rolling down after it. He put them on the rails and then he sat down behind the pile. Not a sound but the wind soughing and rustling in the trees on the ridge above him.

The sound of a little engine. A train was approaching, the lantern up front had already been lit and its light shone on the bare arm of the engine driver who was leaning out. The train was crawling along and when it came near the crossbeams on the track, it halted; he could hear the driver curse as he got off and started dragging them away. Michel ran to the rear at the other side and climbed on an open wagon at the very end.

It was night when they came to a stop at a platform under a metal roof. Across it stood another train, a more serious one with closed freight cars. He tried one door and it slid open, there was straw on the floor and it stank, but nothing stirred. He crept in. When he woke up it was getting light, he pulled the door open and looked straight into the low, rising, sun. They were running south, and quite fast. It was a radiant June morning.

A great calm came over him. I made it, he thought. Out here they hardly know there's been a war on. He sat in the doorway with his feet dangling, and started singing. He hadn't eaten in three days but he felt fine.

Michel, in 1871

5

When they slowed down and houses appeared along the track, he jumped off, he rolled over in the grass and stood up. His ankle hurt but he could walk perfectly. He ducked under the wire that ran along the track at a height of three or four feet, and he stood in a paved street. That wire was the telegraph line to Paris, completed the year before; during the German siege it had been cut, but now the wire traffic had been restored.

The first thing, he thought, is finding out where the hell I am. He followed his street which ran parallel to the railroad tracks and this brought him in a few minutes to the station. Vichy. He was two hundred miles south of Paris and halfway to the Spanish border.

He looked for a while at that name, chiseled in the stone above the entrance. It was funny, because this was the little town his mother had often talked about as the most peaceful, the prettiest, she had ever been in. His parents had lived here in their more prosperous days because the warm springs helped his father's rheumatism. Perhaps Vichy had been the highlight of their marriage. Now, looking at the ladies in long dresses and the men in top hats at this hour of the morning, he could easily imagine his parents among them. (Both his parents had died quite young, before his printing press became well-known, something he had always regretted. Not that his father, an intellectual snob, had been very happy about his son having become an "artisan.")

The passers-by, especially the women, gave him a wide berth: I must look like a tramp, he thought, and I smell. Vichy must have its poor, too, hidden somewhere, I better get there quick, here I stand out like a blight in all this gentility.

He came to a square and saw a plume of dark smoke rising above the roofs, that's for me, that's a factory. Where there's factories the poor live. He soon got to the place, it was a glue-boiling plant and next to it was the slaughterhouse where they'd get their raw material, cow bones. Here the men wore caps and many women went in bare feet. No one stared at him.

He came to a grocery and stopped dead; he had almost walked into a barrel of olives. A sea of smells and colors, greens, fruits, cheeses, rows of sausages and skinned rabbits. A gnawing hunger, which had been kept in check by his thoughts, squeezed his body. He saw himself falling on top of all this stuff and chewing and chewing until they dragged him off. But he stood motionless. I'm not a tramp, I was once a master printer in the capital. He broke one winter carrot off from a bunch, and entered the shop slowly chewing it.

The storekeeper was an elderly man busy sweeping his floor. He leaned his broom against the wall and looked doubtfully at Michel's appearance. "What will it be, young man?" he finally asked.

"I want—to be honest, I am temporarily embarrassed. I left home in such haste, I forgot my purse."

"You are eating one of my winter carrots. They are thirty centimes the pound."

"I'll work for it. If you give me something to eat, I'll work for you this whole day."

"I'll be damned," the man began but then he shrugged. "It so happens—I have all these carts of potatoes sitting in the courtyard. If you unload them and store them in the cellar, neatly mind you, I'll give you a sausage and half a loaf."

"Done," Michel said. "But you must let me eat the sausage first or I'll keel over."

"Not likely. What's to stop you from running off then?"

"I'm a working man. I am your brother."

"You are my brother?"

"Not literally. Like in, liberty, equality, fraternity."

"Fraternity," the man repeated. "That kind of brother. You must be a Parisian."

"No, no. I'm from Vierzon on the Cher, not all that far from here."

"And that's where you left your money this morning?" But then he plucked a sausage from the ceiling and cut Michel a chunk.

It took Michel some hours to get those potatoes down the narrow cellar steps. Once he thought he'd pass out, and he threw up the sausage. But in the end the storekeeper declared himself satisfied, cut some bread, and poured him a glass of wine. "May I have cheese instead of more sausage?" Michel asked.

"Why not. Taste this Marol. Local cheese." He watched Michel eat. "What's your name?" he asked. "I'm monsieur Paul."

"My name is Jules," Michel said.

"Well, Jules, you can come back tomorrow if you want. You can work here till my helper comes back from the army. Two francs a day and your food, and you can sleep in the shack."

"Thank you, monsieur Paul."

Michel was dizzy now, what with the wine and the lack of sleep, but he put his head under the pump in the yard and set off. Monsieur Paul had paid him one franc, and in a tobacco shop he bought an envelope and a sheet of paper, and had the way to the post office pointed out to him. He had more than enough left for a stamp.

"I'm alive, don't give up the ship," he wrote Anne. It was an expression of them, she would know it was him. He signed, "Paul." The address had to be written with a pen, that was a postal rule, but he told the woman at the window he owned nothing but a pencil and it was urgent and very personal, and she brought him a pen and let him dip it in the office ink bottle.

"Are the mails to Paris restored?" he asked her.

"This week anyway. It's really over now."

"Yes, it's over." He smiled at her.

"Madame Anne Beauchamp, 17, Rue Ramponeau, Paris (20th arrond.)" He was about to put his letter in the post box but then decided he had to risk a return address. On the back of the envelope he wrote, "Monsieur Paul, 30, Rue de Paris, Vichy," the address of the grocery store.

Michel, in 1871

6

It would be two weeks before monsieur Paul's helper came back from his guard post at Clermont-Ferrand. That had given Michel time to have a lengthy scrub in the municipal bath house, to eat a number of large meals, and to buy a second-hand jacket in a pawn shop for one franc fifty. The rest of his money he had saved. Monsieur Paul had treated him a number of times to a glass after they closed up, in the café across the street, and Michel (calling himself Jules) had fantasized a past for himself in answer to monsieur Paul's questions. But no reply had come to his letter sent to Anne.

The helper got his job back and Michel went to the glue factory and asked if they had a place for him. The smoke from the glue pots had been his lodestone on his first day and he was a superstitious man who believed in good and bad omens. The factory took him on; boiling glue appeared to be the kind of work no returning soldier wanted. It paid ten francs a week, and a bed in the factory dormitory which was an improvement over the shed. The smell of the place needed getting used to.

Monsieur Paul took him for their glass of wine that evening. "Well, here's to your new job, Jules." He tasted his wine and went on, "Now why would a man like you take a job in that glue place?"

"It's all right."

"You don't suppose I believe you were a farmhand in Vierzon, do you? I've never met a farmhand who speaks like a doctor or a lawyer."

"Oh, I've known better days as they say."

"You know, my friend, I'm an old man and when you saw me first, I was sweeping the floor like a—well, like an old man. But I'm not an old fool."

"I don't think you're an old fool, Paul."

"I'm not. My guess is you're a political fellow and you're in trouble with the government. Either that or you're a police spy." But he smiled while saying that.

Michel smiled back at him. "No, I'm not a police spy and I'm not a political person either. I am a printer or better, I was a printer. But we, Anne my wife and I, are going to start a new and different life."

"Well, Jules, good luck with that."

"Monsieur Paul—Paul—I have to ask you something important. You will get a letter from Paris addressed to you, but it is really for me. Nothing trickish, you can open it, but for God's sake don't give it back to the postman. It is an answer I am waiting for. That's why I'm still in Vichy. You must forgive me for giving your address. I had no other home in this town except your shack."

Monsieur Paul did not look happy with this."Why didn't you ask for an answer addressed to you yourself? You could have written care of Monsieur Paul's grocery."

"Yes—of course—I guess it's that you'd just hired me, I didn't want to presume— I couldn't ask you just then."

"I would have said yes, I'm an easy man. Didn't you tell me we're all brothers?" He smiled again. "I'll keep your letter for you."

Michel Beauchamp, to his own surprise, was at peace among the glue pots. A lowly job seemed fitting for a wanted man. He had definitely not been guilty of any breach of Roman law or Napoleonic law or natural law, yet he felt he could never again be a "respectable citizen," no matter what amnesties and reconciliations might one day be proclaimed. It wasn't opting out what he was doing at the glue factory and he was surely not making some kind of protest gesture there. This is what it was about: in a world such as he had now learned he was living, there was no point in being a printer, nor for that matter a musician or a painter or a number of other *hopeful* professions. Human beings, when the die is cast, don't measure up, they are unable to put themselves in other people's shoes, they are unable to be selfless. I am I and nothing outside my own skin can pain me. It's not nihil humani, *nothing* human, that's alien to me, he thought, but *everything*. If it's that easy to turn our world into a battlefield or a graveyard, at the drop of a hat, you might say, then it's preposterous to worry about Baskerville versus Garamond.

At night, in the factory dormitory where he was the only occupant, those thoughts often turned into nightmares. He was lying on the straw of the army barracks, and the sergeant was reading off the names of the prisoners to be shot at dawn, he read on and on and on. Meanwhile, gray daylight started filtering in through the filthy little windows. Rifle fire echoed. He would wake up in a sweat, still hearing the shots, he'd jump up and go to the window, stare down on the silent and empty street, lit by one flickering gas lantern. He could feel the blood beat in his temples and he whispered, "Anne. Anne. Anne."

THE VERY DAY Michel told monsieur Paul about the letter he was waiting for, his own letter had just reached Paris. It had been stuck for days in Orleans, where the letter sorter of the postal bureau had never come back from the war. The Paris postman took it out the following morning and shoved it under the door of the Beauchamp apartment in the Rue Ramponeau. He was new on the job and didn't know that the Beauchamps had a mailbox with a lock in the courtyard; the regular postman hadn't come back from the war either.

Michel, in 1871

7

The new postman hadn't pushed Michel's letter in far enough, and when he had left the building, the neighbor, Mr Labin, came out of his apartment with a knife and retrieved it.

Michel and Anne had always considered Labin a friendly sort; Michel had done some print work for him once. Labin was a dealer in ivory.

Labin never liked it when they were hugging and kissing; he could look into their kitchen from his kitchen although they weren't aware of that. What interested him was their apartment—obsessed is the better word. He thought it was altogether superior to his own, indeed in a different class, while its rent was only ten francs a month more. Whenever he met them on the stairs, he smiled and lifted his hat, but his only thought was, one day I'll get that apartment of yours.

He had noticed that they had both been absent since the last days of the street fighting and that had given a new slant to his obsession; it legitimized it, so to speak. I knew it, he thought, there was always something fishy about them, for all we know they are arsonists, we don't need people like that in our building. And he had started softening up the owner of the building, he told her that the city was going to requisition all empty apartments for people who had lost their homes in the fires of May (this was a fantasy).

Labin sat down with the letter he had pried out and studied the envelope. He recognized Michel Beauchamp's handwriting, he went through his desk to find an old bill and made sure. Then he opened it. Yes, it was Beauchamp's writing but he signed himself "Paul." Michel and his wife hadn't left together then as he had assumed, and she didn't even know where Michel was. Plus Michel was using a false name and didn't know Anne hadn't stayed home. Now we're getting somewhere, he thought.

Labin's ivory trade had been interrupted by the war but he had savings, he lived alone, and he had nothing to do now but think of his comforts. The German siege, the winter of hunger, and the civil war in the streets had all passed him by. What he knew was that now the ivory trade would soon start up again, and there'd be a lot of pent-up demand.

Every evening he used to go a neighborhood café where he sat for an hour after dinner. That evening, staring at the passers-by without seeing them, an idea struck him which made him half dizzy for a moment. Was it a dirty trick? No, actually it was his civic duty. Was he putting himself in danger? No, for the next ten years no one in his right mind would dare say anything good about the Commune and its friends.

He paid for his beer and set out for the police post of Ménilmontant. That was close to where he lived but not so close that they'd see him go by every day.

He asked for the duty sergeant.

"I've come to inform you of the whereabouts of a Communard," he told the sergeant. "It came into my hands by chance. The man is hiding in Vichy, I have the address."

To his disappointment, the sergeant didn't seem interested. "My dear sir," he said, "we get so many denunciations these days, you wouldn't believe it. We haven't got the time."

"Oh . . . But I bet that they are all anonymous."

"Most of them. Yes."

"Well, you see me standing here, sergeant. I am not anonymous. I am Henri Labin, ivory dealer, of 17, Rue Ramponeau. For five years I was the secretary of the local trade association, the Couronne. You must have heard of it." He waited for a confirmation which didn't come and then added, "I am performing a civic duty here and I expect you to do the same."

Oh God, the jackals, the sergeant thought, but he answered, "Yes, quite. Please give the particulars to our clerk."

Labin went home and burned the letter in his fireplace. The report that the sergeant in Ménilmontant had ended up writing, began its journey to an official in the temporary police headquarters in Versailles. (There had been no great rush back to Paris by the government. The ministers liked their Versailles peace, and the hysteria of the times had greatly exaggerated the damage done to Paris by the rebels. Probably the ministers were also not too eager to face the Parisians who had inspired them with more fear than the Germans ever did.)

Twice a week a mailsack full of reports was dumped on a table in the Versailles police secretariat, and the clerks picked them out haphazardly. Michel had neither good luck nor bad luck; the sergeant's report landed on an official's desk after four days. Of course he could have had the good luck that it would have gotten lost as happened all the time.

But the official who finally got to read, "We have been informed that the Paris printer Michel Beauchamp, a Communard, now hides at 30, Rue de Paris, Vichy, under the name

Paul. No independent verification available," wrote an order for two men to travel there, arrest this Paul, and bring him back.

He could instead have sent a telegram to the police in Vichy but he didn't know the connection had been restored. Moreover, he was hardly more zealous than the Ménilmontant sergeant in cases such as this one.

The lower ranks of the government services were again, as before the civil war, treated like errand boys, but they had to pretend that they had hated the Commune as much as their bosses did.

Michel, in 1871

8

In the night Michel woke up from the rain drumming on the roof and when he came out into the street it was raining hard. The weather had turned. Near the glue pots it was always warm, but at six in the evening, when he quit, it was cold and raining as hard as ever. He had picked up an empty burlap sack to use as a cape over his shoulders and he set out, as had become his routine, for the grocery store to see if his answer had come.

Halfway, on the spur of the moment, he thought he'd go to the post bureau first and ask once more about the service with Paris. He got there a few minutes before closing and the place was empty. He hid his burlap sack in a corner and went to the window. The same woman sat there who had lent him a pen on his visit his first day in Vichy, and he now saw she had short black hair and blue eyes, and was very pretty.

"I bet your name is Françoise," he told her.

"How did you know," she answered with a smile. She had been very bored sitting there, staring at the clock whose hands did not move.

"Listen, Françoise. I've been waiting weeks now for a letter from Paris and it's driving me out of my mind. Is the service restored or not? How long is a letter supposed to take? Could my letter be lost at this office, in some drawer? It was addressed only to 'Paul.' Please help me, it's crucial."

"Ah," she said. "I have a bet, too. It's a letter from a woman."

"It's not what you think. It's very serious."

"And it's 'Paul?' Just that?"

"Paul, 30, Rue de Paris, Vichy."

"I'll go see. Don't go away."

She was gone a long time and he had the sudden feeling she'd found it and would come out waving it with a grin. But she didn't, she came back empty-handed. "There's nothing in the lost-letter box, Paul, and the service is normal, four days at most. Don't look so miserable, now."

"Damn, damn."

"Come now. No swearing on government premises. If you wait a minute you can walk me home. You may share my umbrella."

They passed a café and she said, "Let's have a coffee, I'm cold." But she ordered an anisette liqueur for herself. "I'm shivering, honest," she told Michel. "Here, you ask for a pastis. My treat. You are soaking wet."

Michel looked at the clock over the bar. If he didn't hurry, the grocery would be closed and if the letter had come he wouldn't get it till the next day. But—

"Penny for your thoughts," she said.

"They're not worth a penny. I'm in a quandary. It's too long to explain."

"You sure look better than the first time I saw you. I thought you were a tramp."

"You remember that?"

"Sure. You were already asking about the Paris mails. And you borrowed my pen. Do you work nearby?"

"Yes, at the glue company."

"Are you a demobilized soldier, Paul?"

"Yes. That's what I am. I haven't decided yet what I'm going to do. Glue boiling is just a stopgap."

"I have to go home now," she said. "You don't have to come any further."

"But I'd like to. It's almost stopped raining."

He fished out ten sous but she insisted on paying.

They walked on. Neither of them could think of anything to say. He looked at her, sideways, her profile under the short hair, her hand, a small white hand holding the umbrella, and then the shape of her body, with its very young lines, and the rounding of her blouse—an overwhelming desire got hold of him to kiss and touch that body, she wants me to, otherwise she wouldn't have asked me to come with her—but does this hurt Anne, though she will never know?

"Here we are," she said. "If you want to come in for a moment, you'll get a good coffee. My mom always has the coffee ready." They had come to a halt at the gate of a cottage with a little patch of grass behind a stone wall.

"Your mom?" he asked, swallowing.

"Yes, sure. My father won't be home yet, he works for the railroad."

"Thank you very much. But not tonight, I'm in a bit of a hurry. Another time, all right?"

"Sure, and, I hope your letter will show up soon. I'm sure it will."

He half-ran back to the grocery store but all was locked away and dark there. He cursed himself and turned around.

But as he crossed the road and passed the café where monsieur Paul used to take him for a glass of wine, the man came out. He took Michel by his arm and steered him into a side street. "Let's take a walk," he said.

"What? What's going on, monsieur Paul?"

"We've had visitors today, you and I. Wait till we're on the quay."

"A man showed up in my store today," Paul said, "just before closing. A detective type. He asked if Paul was there. 'I'm monsieur Paul,' I said and he looked very surprised. Had I been in Paris lately, he asked. 'Not in years,' I said, 'I can't leave my store unattended." 'Right,' he said, but did I have someone staying with me, a young man? 'Nobody here but me,' I said. 'I have a helper and he'll be back before closing.'"

"Jules, he made me nervous, that fellow. He started to look around and then he went into the courtyard and I saw him go into the shed. I came after him and I was stopped—at the back door a soldier was standing, a National Guard fellow, and he barred the way with his rifle across my chest, a rifle with a bayonet, if you please—Goddammit, in my own store, I've never . . ." His voice petered out.

"Holy Christ, monsieur Paul—I am so sorry."

"I started to shout and the other man came out of the shed and flashed a card at me, too fast for me to read it. 'Police Nationale,' he said. I never heard of a national police. And then he came into the store and sat down on the only chair, and the chap with the rifle came in and stood by the door. 'Tell him to sheathe his bayonet,' I said. I've been in the army too, you know, very long ago. The detective gave me a vile look and said, 'We're not here to make jokes, get that through your head.' Then my helper came back to close the store with me, and they took him into the yard and talked with him, but for a moment only. He is a bit retarded."

"Damn, damn, damn."

"Yes, you may well say. You were damn lucky, my friend, that you didn't show up just then, as you've been doing every day. I said I had to lock up the store and the detective type said, 'Who's been sleeping in your shed?' 'Oh, an old friend, a nephew from the countryside.' I thought that would be the end of it, but then he told me, 'We'll be back tomorrow morning. And if we find that you have warned off this nephew, we'll arrest you in his place. So you better watch it, you asshole.' That was a government agent, Jules, calling me that." (What the detective actually will have said is, *Vieux con*, old cunt, which is the precise equivalent of our modern "asshole.") "My father was a lieutenant under the Emperor, Jules, in the Grand' Armée. 'Asshole.'"

"I am sorry, monsieur Paul. I have no idea how they could have come after me. It is impossible. It must have been for someone else, some weird coincidence."

"Don't stretch your luck, Jules," monsieur Paul said. "I guess 'Jules' isn't your name either. I can tell you, if he hadn't called me what he did, I might have given the whole show away, I know you are at the glue factory."

Michel remained silent.

"Don't worry, though. I know what to do. But I think you'd better make yourself scarce."

A silence.

"Well, monsieur Paul," Michel finally asked, "What *are* you going to do?"

"I do have a nephew on a farm near here. I'm going there tonight and tell him to come to the store tomorrow, bring me some fresh cheese. That'll get them off my back. Now I'm going home."

Michel sat down on a bench. That post office girl saved my neck, he thought. For tonight I'll be safe in the dormitory. I have to let my clothes dry, get my gear together. I'll be off before it gets light.

But when he came around the corner of the dormitory street, he saw two men in front of the building talking to each other, after which one went inside and the other posted himself across the road. He turned around and walked away, forcing himself not to run.

Ahead of him the street became busy. The sun broke through the rainclouds for a moment and he got his bearings from that: he started to walk as fast as possible, heading south. Soon he came to a bridge which he crossed, and then Vichy already lay behind him. He faced a landscape of fields and woods and he sat down on a rock to catch his breath. Well, here I go again, he said to himself, didn't I proclaim that the wandering life was more real for me now than sleeping in a room and three meals a day? I asked for it. At least I was careful enough to keep my money on me.

But he felt quite miserable, tired, in his wet clinging clothes, and cut off from any sign of life from Anne. He realized that the only possible way they could have traced him to Vichy was through his letter to her. Somehow it must have been intercepted. Anne may never have received it then. He had obviously underestimated the wrath of the government; the chaos of the past weeks had already ceded to the traditional bulldog tenacity of the political police.

The sun set in a skyline of purple clouds which promised more rain, and he started walking again.

Michael, in 1938 and 1939

9

Anne, Michael's grandmother, who died long before he was born, nonetheless had been a big influence on him when he was growing up. She had written a diary, once she was settled in Philadelphia and her child had been born, going back to her lone walk from Paris to Le Havre. Her son, Michael's father, had edited her English a bit (it was quite good really) and had it printed privately. He presented it to his son on his tenth birthday.

Her escape from Paris was already a family legend, and her strong ideas had colored her grandson's concept of the world. Foremost among those, perhaps, was her hatred of the French government, now generalized into a reasoned aversion to all governments and all bureaucratic authority and arrogance. That, and her toughness in adversity and total lack of self-pity.

All this had affected Michael as a boy the more, as his father and mother had always been rather vague and distant to him. They were a self-absorbed and self-indulgent couple. His father, "a man of affairs" as he described himself, had been middle-aged when Michael was born. The local girl he had married, a Kate Wanamaker, traced her family (rightly or mistakenly) to the Main Line Wanamakers, one of Philadelphia's grand families. It would not be unfair to say that as a result those two spent, and wasted, their best years in being expectant, and disappointed, heirs and not much more.

On his eighteenth birthday, when he was in his senior year at his Philadelphia high school, Michael received a legacy of fifteen hundred dollars (a serious sum of money then) coming from his grandmother Anne. His father explained to him that she had asked in her will to set it aside for her first grandson. Michael decided to use it for a stay in Europe. He felt there would be a special meaning attached to being the first Beauchamp repeating Anne's voyage in the opposite direction. A conciliation, perhaps.

He applied for a place at Oxford University but their answer was negative. However, he told his parents (who, anyway, were not used to interfere) that it had all been arranged, and he took passage on a ship to Liverpool. There was an English academic on board who told him about Sheffield University and the very serious degree in geology they offered.

Geology had been his best high school subject and he traveled there straight from Liverpool. They accepted him. That was in the early fall of 1938.

In that year Sheffield had regained its prosperity as a steel town because war was in the air and Britain was rearming. Nonetheless, it was not a cheerful town with its steady days of rain and its streets which died after dark. It affected Michael in a complicated way. Philadelphia High had been a comfortable little nest: its basic philosophy was that, in spite of its ups and downs, life is meant to be good. We can't have everything, but we are entitled to have a lot. Even in a Depression, kids are a privileged minority.

But through the corridors of Sheffield University blew the

icy wind of adult responsibility. Underfed miners' sons on scholarships, faces gray with tiredness, were swotting away (as they called it) to get through their exams, as a failure would have them fall back into a miserable underclass; the sons of the middle classes were forever painfully made aware that Sheffield wasn't Oxford or Cambridge. Michael reacted to all this with detachment; it made him feel strong, free, different. He worked hard, went on lonely walks, and made no friends.

Easter came early in the following year. He had intended to stay put during the holidays, but on the evening of his first day alone in the silent university dormitory, he suddenly jumped up from listening to a lecture on radio BBC-3, threw some things in a satchel, and made it to the late train for London.

On that mild April night, the city came to him as a total surprise. Compared to Sheffield (and even to Philadelphia) it seemed like a northern Naples. Everywhere people were spilling out of pubs and sitting on steps and benches with their drinks. There was a hum of conversation in the air and music came from open doorways. Passing a café or perhaps it was a club, he heard someone in there play a jazz piano. He went in, and that was the end of geology for Michael.

He sat for two hours listening to the pianist, a sickly looking young man. Michael had been to jazz evenings in Philadelphia (on the sly) but he had never heard anyone, black or white, play like that. When the pianist closed the lid and wiped his forehead, Michael went up to him. "What marvelous stuff," he said. "Is it rude to ask where you learned to play like that?"

The man stood up. "I'm going outside," he said. He sat down on a bench out front in the street and lit a cigarette with trembling hands. "I think I have a fever," he told Michael. "Where did I learn— It just came to me like that. Of course I have hundreds of records. Ever heard of Art Tatum?"

"Sure. I'm from America. I had stacks of records too."

"Do you play?"

"Eh, yes. But like an amateur."

"Okay. Why don't you go back in there and play something. I need to sit here a bit and breathe in some clean air."

"You mean—I—"

"Sure, go ahead. They won't bite you. By now they're all in there pissed out of their minds anyway."

Music had played its part in Michael's make-up, from the jazz records he and his schoolmates collected to Mozart operas, taking in Offenbach and Harry James on the way. He now walked hesitantly toward the piano and realized that he hadn't really listened to music or thought about it since leaving the U.S. He sat down in front of the closed piano, afraid to make a fool of himself, afraid of a snide remark from the real pianist who, he saw, had put his feet up outside and sat there smoking his cigarette with his eyes closed.

Then he thought there was a kind of symbolism here, making music now would be in honor of Anne who had sent him on this voyage. He raised the lid and struck a few notes, which made the nearest beer drinkers look up with surprise. And then without analyzing things further, he murmured, "To you, Anne," and started playing "Ain't Misbehavin'."

He had played quite a while before the pianist came back in and put a hand on his shoulder. "Thanks," he said. "You gave me a nice break. And you're not bad. Not good, but not bad. You can stand in for me a couple of hours every night if you want to, till I feel better. Would that suit you?"

"It would suit me very much," Michael answered.

THE MONDAY after Easter Michael sent a telegram to his tutor at Sheffield University that an asthma attack was forcing him to stay away for the rest of the term. Thus followed what he later called for himself, "my fabulous month." He had a room in a boarding house nearby, slept late, walked to the bar in the late afternoon and played whenever the pianist, who was known only by his nickname Poz, decided he needed a rest. He got six shillings a night and never knew if they came from Poz or from the owner. He usually got a free meal at some point in the evening and after a while, when the regulars had gotten used to him, someone or other would put a beer or a whiskey on the piano for him.

Girls came to ask him if he could play this or that, and it happened that he found himself walking one of them home after closing time and being asked in. No great love blossomed from these encounters but they cured loneliness and other miseries with "the balm you can't buy in the pharmacy," as Zerlina sings in "Don Giovanni."

The music was the happiest thing. From being a dilettante he had of a sudden become a professional of sorts, part of the show, as when friends of the pianist showed up and they all sat together and talked about jazz, and someone might even ask him about the way things were in the U.S. And there was an edge to life then and there, because of a sense that the party would soon be over, and end in war.

But then Poz had to go to hospital and a new pianist was hired who didn't need or want him. Michael started making the rounds of other bars and clubs but people didn't even ask him to let them hear something, and in a short time he was broke, one pound in his pocket and his room not paid. He brooded about writing or wiring his parents but couldn't do it, he had written them too many fantasies—well, lies, to be precise.

On one of those walks of his he passed a queue of young men waiting at the army recruiting station newly opened on the Strand. He stopped, and then he went to stand in line.

An hour later he had been signed up as a new member of His Majesty's armed forces.

He thought it would also be an ironic but good way to set foot in Anne's France, as an Allied soldier.

Michael, in 1941

10

In the bar "Chez Jo" in Vichy, Michael was taking little sips from his wine to make it last longer. He had to choose his next move. Go back to the American legation in the Villa Ica and apologize? If he played it humble enough he might get to see a higher-up. But then? "Our hands are tied," he could hear them say it. There had been a Scot in his POW camp who regularly harried him about his country's neutrality. The evening before Michael's escape the man had assured him that the Americans in Vichy were buddy-buddy with Pétain and his jolly band of pro-German collaborators. Well, maybe the guy was right.

I've got sixteen francs left, he thought, I'll go to the railroad station and get a third-class ticket to the farthest place south it'll buy, and then I'll just start walking to the Spanish border. Franco, yes, not so great, but the man stayed out of it in 1940 after all, and he'll be even more neutral now in his fashion. People on trains are always stuffing themselves, someone will offer me something. So I'll just beg or steal if need be. Hanging out in this town will get me in jail for certain. So come on, Mike, buck up.

Michael got to the station by nightfall. It was filled with men, women, and children, crying and shouts, bundles, people sitting and lying on every horizontal space. This town, Vichy, had gone from a little resort with medicinal springs to being the capital of half of France, and now it had room for VIPs only. Michael warily made his way to a ticket window. It was closed and along the wall a long line of men and women waited for it to reopen. Those in front looked on with a certain glee when he knocked on the window, unaware of the line. When he took it in, he felt so worn out that he made his way to a far corner where he found a few square feet to lie down, and instantly fell asleep.

Angry voices woke him up. It was pitch-dark now, with one far-off lightbulb painted blue. But flashlights were being used nearby, and he realized two policemen were waking up people and demanding to see their papers. He crawled away.

He came to a narrow corridor with a row of doors, all locked. The glass in the last door was broken, he could just distinguish the crack which reflected a glimmer of light from somewhere. He pushed his elbow through the glass which easily shattered, and then he could reach the doorknob from the inside.

It turned out to be an office with a window on the street, from which that scrap of light came. He was hard up to use the toilet; if you got to go you got to go, he said to himself, and he squatted behind a filing cabinet for the purpose. He wiped himself with some papers from the desk.

Sorry folks, disgusting, I know, but so is being shot disgusting. There's a war on. What's really amazing is not any breakdown of society here, but to the contrary, how people pretend, how they go on as before. They're more at ease now with the Germans than with all those freaks who want to continue the war, the English pilots, the guys from the Resistance. The Germans are the routine now, the status quo, the other guys disturb the peace. How we all cling to any kind of security, imagined or not. Well, that's some philosophy in exchange for smelling up your office.

At first light Michael went to stand in the ticket line and an hour later he had a ticket for Nîmes, changing trains in Avignon. "How old are you, sir?" the clerk had asked him and for an agonizing moment he couldn't think in French before he muttered, "Vingt ans," twenty, and the man gave him a reduced fare.

When the train pulled into the station, an hour late, he lost out in the scramble for seats but eventually he found a space to squeeze in half his backside. It was a long day and all around him people were unwrapping chicken legs, sausages, cheese, bread, but no one offered him a thing. Fucking black marketeers, he told them silently. Avignon was the final stop of this train and by then it was dark again. When the people around him had gone, he fished out a bag with chicken bones someone had shoved under the seat. He had kept an eye on it for the past hour and now he gave the most promising bones another go. Then he got off.

On a time-table on the wall, covered with scribbled names and dirty words, he found the train to Nîmes. Leaving at midnight. He spent as much time as possible studying the poster next to it which proclaimed "Travail, Familie, Patrie." "Travail" doesn't mean "suffering" as in English (which would be appropriate all right) but "work." As a slogan it didn't really beat "Liberté, Egalité, Fraternité," he decided. Above the text a sheepish Marshall Pétain held out his hand (gloved) to a gangly young man and a Gretchen-type girl who were shouldering spades as if they were rifles. He looked around for something else to read or while away the time with, but everything was dark, closed, boarded up. On the positive side, there were no crowds here, hardly a soul.

Finally, finally, the Nîmes train came in which was filthy and had wooden benches, looking like an exhibit in a railroad museum. But he fell asleep, and slept right through the Nîmes stop, waking up in Montpellier.

Alarm: if he'd show his Nîmes ticket at the exit, and with no money to pay the extra cost, he'd be in deep trouble. He tried the exit door to the tracks, but it was locked.

Two elderly, tired-looking, women boarded the train with mops and buckets, and began their work by collecting refuse from under the benches. He hastily took off his jacket, picked up a bucket and a broom which he shouldered like a Pétain volunteer and marched down the platform and out the exit.

MICHAEL, IN 1941

II

MONTPELLIER WAS A PRETTY LITTLE TOWN IN THE STILL, cool, morning. No feeling of war here, Michael thought, and he became unaccountably happy. He saw himself walking along, in a complete anonymity, dizzy with hunger, but fit, feeling good. He caught his reflection in a shop window. The south of France, a thousand miles away from the gray *schnell, schnell* camp and its fat-assed corporals counting us from morning till night. This, what I'm about here, is a good adventure. It's about dealing with people, friend and foe, not about dealing with machines, not a machined adventure such as our raid on the French coast.

What was adventurous about that? The only question asked was, is some guy who can barely see me, going to kill me or miss me or castrate me or paralyze me. A matter of an inch to the left, an inch to the right. Some adventure.

In a decent adventure you need contrast and variation like in nature. Not an all-male adventure either, you must deal with men and women. And animals, once, but that's no longer on.

And from thinking that, he focused on a woman walking in front of him, a young woman in a straight, sack-like dress of wrinkled linen, bare legs, and shoes which were blocks of wood with straps. These had come into use because leather had vanished, but he didn't know that. He thought her outfit looked funny, funny playful, anti-war, anti-orderliness, anti-German. She even walked in a rebellious way. As he passed her, he gave her a furtive look and a smile, but he didn't pause for any reaction.

At the street corner ahead of him he noticed a slowing down and a thickening in the mass of pedestrians, and he became aware of a tension in the air. He saw caps of policemen sticking out, one, two, and one on the corner across the street. "A control," someone near him muttered. So much for "no war" in Montpellier.

And then he felt a hand on his arm and discovered it was the woman on the clogs. "Help me through," she whispered.

Oh God. That's what comes from smiling at strangers. "I'm not a good bet," he whispered back.

She stopped, people went around them, they were about twenty feet from the policemen. Any moment they would be noticed. "Please," she said quite loudly.

Oh well. "I am Joseph Auteuil," he whispered, putting his arm around her waist, and they walked on like lovers in a trance, ignoring their surroundings.

There were actually three policemen on their side of the street, blocking the sidewalk. Studying them he steered for the middle one, whose face wasn't more sympathetic but more phlegmatic, more bored. Looking at this man, Michael told himself, I'm on top of the situation, I'm a trained soldier.

The policeman held out his arm sideways and they stood still. Then Michael grinned and gave the man an idiotic bow, a bow as he remembered from a film version of "The Three

Musketeers." He presented his Joseph Auteuil identity card with a flourish, and pushing up the girl's chin, he said, "Joseph Auteuil at your service, and here is my little wife Jane Auteuil." For "wife" he used the word "épouse" which he thought had a comic connotation for such a young girl.

It all worked. The officer had a ghost of a smile for all this vivacity or possibly he liked the touch of cruelty with which Michael pushed the girl's face up at him, and he turned to the next person, a man who was already searching his pockets with a puzzled frown, or a fake-puzzled frown.

When they had rounded the corner, they started to walk very fast until they were quite a distance away.

"You did that well," she said. "Thank you, sir."

The color had come back in her face and now it had a most appealing freshness.

"I admit I'm pleased with myself," Michael said. "Whenever I heard about this kind of thing, I've always thought, if you just simply feel, 'How dare they, the hell with them,' they will recognize that, they'll be, well not exactly afraid of you, but—"

He stopped because she was looking at him with a skeptical half-smile. She said, "—Ah." She held out her hand. "Again, many thanks."

"Wait," Michael said. "Do you have any money?"

"What?"

"I mean, for a cup of coffee. I've no money—on me. Let's sit down for a moment and, well, catch our breath."

She gave him a thoughtful look. "All right."

They crossed the street to a café terrace and took the farthest table. A boy in a white apron brought them two cups of a dark liquid.

"I'm not Joseph Auteuil," Michael said.

"You're not French, I can hear that now."

"I'm an American."

"That explains it."

Michael tasted his coffee, it burned his mouth but he drank it all. It stopped his stomach from grumbling.

"Well," he answered her, "as you just saw, I managed. I was taught."

"Taught? Where?"

"In the army, a special school for—"

"My friend," she interrupted, switching to an only slightly accented English, "you must be kidding. I assure you, if this had happened in Paris, with two *Feldgendarmen* asking for our papers, there would have been no smiles. We'd be on our way to the Gestapo."

"Ah, well, yes, the *Feldgendarmerie*—although—But what have they got against you?"

She didn't answer. She stood up. "Again, my thanks."

"You haven't drunk your coffee. Do you live in this town?"

She shook her head.

"Are you all alone here?"

She hesitated, and shrugged. "Yes."

"Don't you trust me?" he asked.

"I trust no one. Not even myself. This is a fucking world to find yourself in. What a waste, to be young now."

He laughed, because of her using the word "fucking" and because she pronounced it as if it rhymed with "looking."

Her face changed, it was as if it were folding, as if her head was in a press. She looked haggard suddenly, but like a child. She sat down again.

"Listen, Mary," he said. "May I call you Mary?"

"Sure. Since it isn't my name."

"Mary—I'm not afraid of those bastards. Don't you be either."

"The difference between you and me, dear sir, is that if you get caught with the wrong papers, or no papers, they'll put you in jail—maybe—for a week, or even for a month. But then your consul drives up in his Dodge automobile and gets you out . . ." Her voice dwindled.

"And if you get caught?"

"If I get caught, I'm dead."

Michael looked pleased. "You're in the French Resistance. I hoped for that. I hoped to run into someone like that."

She shook her head. "No. Nothing heroic."

"Then why?"

"Oh for God's sake," she cried, exasperated now. She turned her pocketbook over above the table and shook everything out, a handkerchief, a comb, a lipstick, a mirror, a wallet—no keys.

"Here," she said. "My carte d'identité."

Next to her picture on the card a large black J had been stamped. "I'm a student at the Sorbonne. I'm from Holland," she said hurriedly. "I can't go back, my father got arrested. My mother got away, she dived under, on a farm." She had a little smile. "That's translated Dutch for if you go underground in Holland. That's how wet the ground is. As for me—I escaped from the French-occupied zone. And now I'm stuck."

He stared at her card with the black J. "This isn't simple harassment," he said. "This is deadly, it's their first step."

"You don't say."

"It's like how they mark trees where I come from. They come back later and cut them down."

"Yes. Now can we change the subject?" She took a sip from her cup and put it down.

"If you don't want it, I'll drink it," Michael said. "I'm dying of thirst."

The girl started throwing her possessions back into her pocket-book.

"I'm on my way to Spain," he announced. "Why don't you come along?"

"Just like that?"

"Just like that."

"To go to Spain, one is needing, I mean in need of, a valid residency card for the unoccupied zone of France, an exit permit from the Germans, and most impossible of all, a Spanish visa. I assume you have all those?"

"Not a one."

"You're not funny, sir."

"Michael. Michael Beauchamp. My family comes from France originally. There is a family story, a myth perhaps, that we—"

"Michael. Please. As I said before, for you all this may be a boys' adventure. For me, it's bang." She held her finger against her head and fired an imaginary bullet.

"For your information, Mary, the Fuhrer has ordained that all commandos caught in my raid who now try to escape, are to be executed. So the camp commander reminded us every morning at roll-call."

She stared at him and turned pale. "You're an escaped commando?"

"Yes."

"And American?"

"Yes. But in the British army. Seven Troop, Four Commando."

"I don't believe you."

For answer he unbuttoned his shirt. Around his neck he wore British Army identification tags. "Name, religion for when you die, they take the red one and leave the green octagonal one. Read it. Michael Beauchamp, W/Sgt."

"Put that back! Button your shirt!"

"We're not going to be pushed around, you and I, Mary."

She shook her head, silently. After a while she asked, "What does 'C of E' mean?"

"That you get a nice funeral with music. If they find you, and if they have the time. Look, Mary—"

"And what about the Spaniards? Franco's police?"

"We'll tell them you're American too."

"And they'll say, 'Of course, welcome, señorita americana.'"

"Look," Michael said, "Do you swear loyalty to the flag, one nation under Roosevelt, and so forth and so on?"

She had regained control of herself and laughed. "Okay," she said with a heavy imitation American accent, holding up her hand. "I swear."

"You're now an American. What's your real name?"

"Marie. I mean, Mary."

"Mary, pour l'amour de Dieu, do you have any money to spare, to buy something to eat?"

Marie, in 1939 and 1940

12

In 1938 Marie de Jongh was a first-year student at the university of Leyden. She was only just seventeen. There was a threat of war in the air and Dutch army conscripts were in garrisons along the borders; many students were on reserve duty and attended the lectures in uniform. But Holland had been neutral for a long time and life went on normally.

Marie was a pleasant-looking girl, still a bit gawky but quite beautiful at times, especially when wearing a large hat as she liked doing, or by candlelight. She was a virgin as was almost a matter of course then. (That year there was a *rumor* at the university that one of the female first-years was no virgin: this illustrates how things were in those days).

Her first year disappointed her. Academic history was not the intriguing subject she had expected it to be. She was bright, she wrote a paper on the Paris Commune which made some original points— no small feat on a subject which had been chewed over by droves of professors for the past ten years. On the strength of it she was offered a year at the Sorbonne University of Paris in an exchange program, which she immediately accepted.

Thus when the war did break out in 1939, she was already ensconced in a room of her own at the student house in the

Rue de l'Université. Her parents wrote to her that she should come home, but in France life also went on near normally and they agreed that she could wait and see.

Marie's father had started out as a family doctor in the town of Rotterdam but he was now an archivist at Keesing's, a publisher of medical documentations. He had to travel a lot and claimed that he wasn't really an archivist but a poet although of course that wouldn't pay the rent. There was a lot in his poems about the better world of the future and the horror of tyranny and war, and he was often a speaker at congresses of the Dutch Labor Party which in the thirties was radical.

When he and his wife were sitting in their living room in Amsterdam at night, with not a sound coming from the empty streets outside, she would sometimes put down her book and say, "What if it comes here, Jan?" And Jan would mutter, "Never fear" without losing his place in the evening newspaper.

"It" was the national socialism of Holland's neighbor Germany, and Jan de Jongh was Jewish.

On May 10, 1940, at six in the morning, the doctor's wife came into his study where he was fiddling with a poem before going to work, and announced, "Jan, they've invaded us. We are at war with Germany."

At that time most people expected that a frontline would emerge between the German armies and the French and British ones, just as had happened in 1914. Marie, in Paris, registered as a nurse's aide for an army hospital, but they seemed to have no use for her anywhere. Then, as the Germans came nearer, she decided to go to England and try there. She actually got herself on a train to Calais but after an hour there came an air raid alert, the train stopped, and the passengers were told that was the end of the line.

She went back to Paris against the stream of the refugees from the city who had now begun their big exodus, and for two weeks she was the only student in the university house. When classes started again, it was in a Paris occupied by the Germans.

In Holland, De Jongh was arrested and sent to a concentration camp. The Germans had arrived with a blacklist of their enemies, leftists and "political Jews" and De Jongh qualified on both counts. His wife would have been taken too, but she was away and a friendly neighbor warned her off. She journeyed on a borrowed bicycle to a farm on the island of Walcheren south of Rotterdam. The farmer was a family friend; long ago he had been a patient of De Jongh and they had stayed in touch. He took Mrs. de Jongh in. Through the same neighbor who had warned her not to come home, she got a message to the Sorbonne for Marie, that there was a safe place at the farm for her too.

But Marie did not want to make herself a refugee in hiding, she wanted to get into the war.

The general feeling at the time in France was that the war was lost and over, and that England would very soon be knocked out too. But in London De Gaulle started his broadcasts and presently some few military officers and some politicians escaped from occupied France and joined him.

Various other groups organized themselves in secret to help people get to England, escaped prisoners of war, and volunteers for the British or French or Polish or Dutch armies which were all being rebuilt. But they weren't willing to take the great risks involved, just to send a young girl without any military or warlike use.

Michael, in 1941

13

NEXT TO THEIR CAFÉ TERRACE WAS A BAKER. MARIE turned out to have three hundred francs, and they got two baguettes of bread without coupons for five francs. They went to a second-hand clothes shop of which there were many in those days, Michael stuffing chunks of bread in his mouth as they went along. Marie bought an old peasant woman's black dress but it made her look more like a high school girl going to a party than like a farm woman. Michael got a dark blue blouse such as farmers and mechanics wore, and still wear, in France.

"I have a suitcase with clothes and books," she told Michael, "all I own is in there. It's at the dormitory for working women where I slept last night. Can I go get it?"

"If you must. I think you shouldn't."

She considered this. "All right, I won't."

"Good for you, Mary. You'll see how light and free it makes you feel. And you won't believe how many people get caught just because they had to go back for one more thing. And now there's only one thing I still want from this town, a map."

But in the bookstore they were told by the owner that area maps weren't for sale any more, only maps on a scale of one to a million. A German decree. "You see, sir, you must admit, the

Germans if they're anything, they're thorough.'"

"They sure are."

"And, sir, madam, when all is said and done, maybe it's all for the best for France. After all those slipshod years we've gone through, strikes and sit-ins by the Reds and all the rest of it."

"Long live slipshod," Michael said.

"What an old devil," she said when they were outside.

He shrugged.

"And he smelled horrible, too. Like that cheese they wouldn't give us without ration coupons." She giggled but she had tears in her eyes.

At the railroad station they tried to buy tickets to the town of Perpignan, which is only twenty miles from the Spanish border, but the clerk told her such tickets could be sold only to passengers holding border zone permits. "But we have those," Marie assured him. "We just didn't bring them."

The clerk looked bored and remained silent.

"We'll go get them, we'll be back in a flash."

"You'll still have to go back in line, miss."

Instead they went south on a local bus. It was still running twice a day, not on gasoline but on methane stored on the roof in a big rubber sack. "It seems to stop at every farm," Michael said.

"At every cow."

They sat in the back, with not much to say. They smiled when they caught each other's eyes. "You trust me now?" he asked.

"Eh—yes."

But they only got as far as Narbonne, where the bus broke down in front of the local café. Another bus would come, the passengers were informed, but it would take a couple of hours, and people settled themselves, on the benches in front of the church, in the grass by the side of the road, and on the terrace of the little café. The road in front of them lay abandoned in the summer sun, not a car or a human being appeared on it.

The café was part of a hotel, a miserable looking place with a rusty sign, "Running water. Modern comforts." "Let's go here," Michael said. "The Lion of Gold, you can't lose with a name like that."

"I thought we were going to sleep in haylofts. That'll be a lot cleaner."

"Yes, but so near the border, if the cops go by, they pick you up. And I want a bath. I need one."

"Okay then, but only if they have a real bathroom, and hot water."

They went in and looked around but there was no one there. Behind the house they found a woman cleaning vegetables. "Yes of course there is hot water," she said. "You think we are pigs here?"

No, they didn't think that, Michael assured her. They needed two rooms, they were brother and sister. "That'll be twelve francs—if you share a room, you'll be better off."

"Yes, but no, rather two."

(They didn't for a moment consider sharing a room, they were both exhausted and didn't want to deal with the arranging that would have required. They got on well now, as if they had been friends for a long time. There was nothing sexual man-woman about it; Michael would have been mortified if she had thought he was after her. He thought she was marvelously appealing, but precisely because the whole hotel-room-sharing business was so corny and obvious, it was unthinkable to try and use it.)

Michael, 1941

THE FOLLOWING MORNING they were both up at first light and went downstairs together. Marie looked at him and began to laugh. "We're like an old married couple."

"More like father and daughter."

"How old are you, Michael?"

"Twenty. Twenty-one soon."

"It all seems so calm here," Marie said.

"I know. Humdrum. Boring."

"Ha ha. Actually—I lay awake most of the night. A mild panic attack."

"It's okay, Mary. It's okay. All will be okay. Do you know what a *passeur* is?"

"But for sure. There was a bar in Montpellier where it was a regular market of them."

"But—"

"But they asked thousands of francs, and jewelry, and gold watches. I got talking with the bar woman and she assured me that often they pretend they'll take their clients across the border and then they sell them to the Gestapo instead."

Michael shook his head. "Yes, but that's a different species. There are others, Resistance types, and they don't do it for money, they help downed pilots and escaped POWs. And I, I dear Mary, have the name of one of them. In Perpignan. He used to be a regular smuggler before the war, a professional, he passed an army pal of mine across the border of Spain, after Dunkirk."

"And you know he's still there?" There was a tremor in her voice.

"I'm sure. And even if he isn't. I'm a commando, young lady. I know about terrain and cover and sight lines. I'll walk us across all right, no fucking fear."

The woman had brought them bowls of chicory and bread, and they paid her and walked to the bus stop. "Twenty minutes," Michael said, looking at the timetable.

As they stood there, a horse and cart passed by and the farmer slowed down and shouted something they didn't understand. Marie hurried after him. He stopped and they talked for a moment.

"What was that about?" Michael asked.

She sat down on the bench at the bus stop and started to cry.

"Oh no," Michael said. He sat down beside her and put his arm around her. "Come on, Mary. Please don't collapse."

"It—it took me a while to get it. It's horrible French they speak here. Or maybe it's excellent Catalan."

"Well?"

"It's Sunday, Michael. The bus doesn't run any more on Sunday."

"So—so we'll have a day off. We're pretty safe here. I'll go tell her we keep the rooms one more day."

She shook her head and swallowed and started sobbing again. "I'm so tired," she finally managed to say. "I've been on the run for so long now—if you hadn't picked me up yesterday, I think I'd have cut my wrists that evening."

The thought went through his mind, I shouldn't have gotten involved with her. She'll slow me down or, God knows, she'll screw us up.

She wiped her face with the sleeve of her black dress and looked at him with her strange eyes, not brown, he now saw, they were gray, pewter gray, grey with an e the way they spell it in England, our gray with an a is too red—poor girl, what a pathetic face, but she is a beauty all the same, even right now. "Mary, Mary," he whispered. "It'll be all right."

He walked her down to the center of the little town, Rue Jean Jaurès, the main street. They were so far south now that the shops didn't have doors but bead curtains, there was as little for sale in the windows as up north but under the bright blue sky and with the black and white pattern of sun and shade on the sidewalks it looked cheerful nonetheless.

"It's hard to believe that you can starve in this climate," Marie said, "But you can, people do." She fell silent, she had become aware of a buzz in the air, people congregating in little groups, voices louder than normal. "Something is going on," she said nervously. "Do you notice?"

He took her arm and steered her into a bar-tabac. "We're out of cigarets," the woman behind the counter automatically announced.

"Oh—but what's going on in town?"

She peered suspiciously at them. "What? Nothing is going on."

"People seem excited, sort of," Marie said.

"Oh, that. Because of Russia, I guess."

"What about Russia?"

"But—the war. Monsieur 'itler has invaded them."

"No kidding!"'

She shrugged. "That man, he never stops. But he is strong, no? Four weeks. That's all it will take him."

"How about a pack of Gauloises for the occasion?" Michael asked.

"But I told you already. None left."

Outside, Michael picked up the girl and whirled her around. "Hurrah!" he shouted very softly. "A big day, Mary. He's given up on his invasion of England. Four weeks my ass. He's lost his war, monsieur 'itler."

"But it'll be a long while."

"Yes."

"And the Russians are bastards too. That pact."

"Do you know who Neville Chamberlain was?" he asked.

"Are you serious? Michael, I'm a Sorbonne history major."

"I keep forgetting. You look too young. I was in London when old Neville came back from Hitler and waved his pact. I don't see how the Ruskies had any other choice."

"But we were all so happy then. My father phoned from somewhere, I forget, very far, he was so relieved. And the students—"

"Yeah. They were all very wrong though, weren't they."

"Well, we all had an extra year."

TOWARD EVENING it cooled off beautifully. The sun was setting in a band of color. His feeling of confidence that he'd make it, his sudden belief, no, certainty of that—the war which would be won—whatever it was, his spirit flew up. His happiness was contagious, she pressed his hand and beamed at him.

They started walking back to the hotel. The sun dipped under the horizon; "The hour between dog and wolf," she said. "Did you know that's what they call it here? Entre chien et loup."

"I like that. And in a while it will be l'heure blue, I know that from an ad."

"Let's go to bed," she answered.

Her room in the little hotel was unexpectedly light and airy. "She gave you a much better room than me," he said.

"But of course."

He sat in the windowsill and she stood beside the bed, then

in two or three movements she had all her clothes off and jumped on the bed, pulling the cover up over her.

He muttered something and went out into the corridor to find a toilet.

When he was back in the room, he was too embarrassed to look at her and he went back to the windowsill.

"How old are you really, Michael?" she asked.

"Twenty. Almost twenty-one."

"And you're a sergeant in the British army?"

"Acting slash war-substantiated. That means the lowest of the low sergeants."

"Nevertheless. Neanmoins. Take your clothes off and come here."

Then she told him, "Stand still and drop that shirt. I'm not going to buy a pig in a poke. I want to look at you first."

Among the experiences Michael had in the Lion d'Or, one was the discovery that it is vastly exciting to stand still, naked, with a woman looking hard at you.

They had a night, a day, and a night in that room. They went out to buy food and they spent sixteen of her francs on four hot baths, two each. The war was over and won, *Ausweise* was a word of the past, they'd forgotten the name of the town outside the window. What Michael thought of was her body, its softness and roundness, the way her skin resisted the pressure of his hands, and of his own body of which he was more aware than he had ever been before.

Later he sometimes felt that those thirty-six hours were all that they'd had together, their only reality. Or conversely, during the very bad times, they seemed unreal, an erotic fantasy.

Michael, in 1941

14

The bus to Perpignan showed up. Michael climbed aboard first, paid for two, and went all the way to the back. The driver didn't even look at him and certainly wasn't interested in travel permits or in fact in anything else. Michael carried only his raincoat; his shaving things and a pair of underpants were in the pockets. To his surprise the bus was almost empty. Marie got on and fell down next to him as the bus suddenly took off.

It was a gray morning. She scrutinized him and began to laugh. "You're very pale," she said.

"It is the light."

"It's too much screwing. Poor boy."

"Mary. Wash your mouth."

"You're shocked, are you?"

"I'm a product of a British university. Well, two semesters."

"That just means buggery in cold dormitories."

"You know too much."

"And you're too romantic." She closed her eyes for a moment and whispered, "Bon voyage." He held up his hands with his fingers crossed.

There were many stops and the bus began to fill. The day

remained dull, they rattled through a poor, barren, landscape but then there were glimpses of water, come and gone, through the bus windows across the aisle from them: the Mediterranean. Gray water with glittering white foam on the waves. He thought there was something ominous about it. Maybe we're on a death ride.

"What is it?" she asked.

"Nothing. An angel walked over my grave or whatever the expression is."

"Shall I tell you my life's story?"

He smiled at her. "Here we go, and I don't even know your name."

"Marie de Jongh. Marie is *the* name for Dutch girls, like Jan for boys. My mother is also a Marie. I like it when you call me Mary. And I went to Greycoat Hospital in London which is not a hospital but a girls' school and to the Barlaeus Gymnasium in Amsterdam which is not a gym but a Latin school. And you know my father is in a concentration camp. We hope. Perhaps he is dead. And my mother is hiding out on a farm. And then I met this strange American, just as I was about to give up. Michael . . . are we just whistling in the graveyard?"

"No whistling. We're outwitting them."

It was not yet midday when the bus reached Perpignan. They had thought it would take all day. Here they were standing in a busy town square and watched the driver lock the bus and vanish into a café as the clock in the church tower started striking twelve.

They weren't happy at all about this speed; they had counted on another night without having to think about the border yet. "But we're actually damn lucky," Michael discovered, "What were we thinking of? This isn't Narbonne, it is a real town with real cops checking the hotel registers. And too close to that damn border to mess with sleeping in haylofts. Let's get out of here. Bread and apples, and find the passeur."

"What's his name?"

For an unnerving moment he couldn't think of it. "Pierre! Pierre Brossolette, in the Cataline bar."

It took time to find the place. It was a dump but a large one. They didn't even seem to have electricity in there, there was one oil lamp and the back of the room was lost in the shadows. The only person on hand was the man behind the bar who was smoking a cigarette rolled in a piece of newspaper.

"Two coffees please," Michael asked.

"Haven't had coffee in here since Christmas 1940. Barley."

"Two barleys. And we have a question for you."

"Ah," the man said, from the depth of his experience that no one entered the Cataline without an ulterior motive.

"Do you know where we can find Pierre?" Michael thought he was clever phrasing it that way.

"Pierre? Just Pierre?"

"You know, the Pierre, Pierre Brossolette."

"Never heard of him."

Michael drank his barley coffee without making a face, for the cause so to speak. Perhaps that pleased the man behind the counter, "Who's asking?" he inquired.

"I'm Michel. This is my wife Marie. Pierre's niece lives with us in Bordeaux."

"So what are you after here?"

"We're on a walking tour." Oh shit, he thought, looking at the man's face, that was stupid.

"A walking tour. That must be nice."

"Let's get out of here," Marie whispered.

"You know, you don't sound French to me," the man told Michael, "I've an ear for that. I've worked on ships, ten years, on freighters, you get to meet the devil and his grandmother. You wouldn't be a German by any chance?"

"No."

"Not, mind you, that there's anything wrong with being German."

"Well, I'm glad you think so, because yes, I'm a German. I've come to raid this place, to arrest all those foreign agents in the corner there drinking champagne. No, I'm not a fucking German. I'm not a fucking Frenchman, I'm not even a fucking Jew. All right?" He took Marie's hand and pulled her with him.

"Hold your horses, fellow. Some calm. Why don't you turn right when you get out of here. A couple of houses down, on this side. Place with green curtains. They may know something. The barley is eighty centimes."

The woman of the green curtains did know. "Pierre has moved to Le Boulou."

"Where is that, madam?"

"Le Boulou. You don't know where Le Boulou is?"

"No, we don't."

"You're not from here then?"

"No. We aren't."

"Le Boulou is to the south. On the Nationale nine."

"Far?"

"I've never gone there. Couple of hours walking, I'd say."

"Isn't there a bus?"

"A bus? No, there's no bus. You people aren't from here, I guess."

"No, we're not, madam," Marie said. "We're from Bordeaux."

"Bordeaux! Then you can't go to Le Boulou. Military zone."

So they bought some apples and a cake, since they couldn't get bread, and started walking.

It turned out to be a very long way. The sun was getting low when they saw in the distance roofs of buildings, farms, and presently they came to the blue-on-white town sign, Le Boulou. But next to it sat a large sign in the German colors, black, white, and red, which in two languages proclaimed a military zone, *verboten* for people without the special residents' permits.

From where they stood, they could see a guard house at the entrance of the village street. It looked empty but they both had the same idea, not to be conspicuous, and they immediately turned right on a path that met the Nationale on their side of the no-entry notice.

They ended up in the large courtyard of a farm, with a dog on a chain barking at them in a mad rage, and a man in city clothes who had been busy washing an old Renault, taking off his work gloves and coming up to them.

"We are looking for Pierre Brossolette," Marie said.

"Why don't we go in." The man led them into the farm kitchen where they sat down at a long wooden table. He poured himself a little glass from a bottle of liqueur on the table but didn't offer any. "What you want with Pierre?" he asked.

Marie opened her mouth to come up with some kind of answer but in the meantime he had turned his back on her and cut himself a chunk of cheese on a sideboard. "Yes?" he asked without turning.

"I'm an army officer," Michael said. "I was a prisoner. Pierre has helped a friend of mine across the border here. Could you, or someone here, tell him to come and see us? Can we pay someone to take a message to him in Boulou?"

"Of course we could do that. But Pierre is away, you see."

"Are you sure?" Michael asked.

The man sat down again and stared at them without answering. "Yes, Pierre sure knew the region," he finally said. "But he's not the only one."

A silence.

This guy is dangerous, Michael thought. We're not handling this right.

"Can you help us?" Marie asked abruptly.

"Well, help—help—I'm a businessman, you realize, not like Pierre."

"Of course. You should be paid for your time."

"It's more than time, young lady. And there's the car. You easily pay a hundred francs for a liter of gas nowadays."

"*How much*?" Marie asked. And to Michael, who was shaking his head at her, she said, "To hell with all this fencing, Michael. I can't do another step."

"We're not rich," Michael informed the man.

"Ha, ha," he laughed. "They all say that."

They all say that. Rich Jews, he means. Michael stood up.

"We own exactly two hundred francs," Marie announced.

"You can't be serious, young lady. Two hundred francs? I'd spend more on the gasoline."

"You can have my watch," she said. "It belonged to my mother. It's a Patek Philippe."

"Let me see it." He took a long time studying it.

"Here's my watch too," Michael said. "And that's all we have. Take it or leave it."

The man got up and put the two watches in a little drawer of the kitchen cabinet. "Frenchmen should help each other," he informed them. "We'll go at nine tonight. You can wait here."

THEY DROVE OFF in the asthmatic Renault. The man, whose name they never learned, drove with no lights but in the long summer twilight the dirt road was easy to follow. They didn't stay on it long, he turned off and they bounced along on a path of earth and loose stones, trees on both sides, until they came to a clearing. The man turned the car around and stopped. "Here we get out. Follow me."

It was dark under the trees and hard to see where to put your feet. They stumbled along on the stony ground. The only sounds came from the wind and very far off a dog was barking. "This is as far as I go," he announced. "Go straight on, and when you come to a farm house, the ruins of a farmhouse, you're in Spain."

He turned. "Wait one moment," Michael cried, "this is not what we agreed on."

But the man had already vanished in the dark and a few seconds later they heard the car start and drive off. Then all was quiet until of a sudden a dog barked quite close by.

"Oh Michael." Marie put her arms around him.

"I knew he was a bastard. Never mind, let's go, hold on to my raincoat."

They half ran, half stumbled along, the trees got sparser and the ground more rocky. He thought that was a good sign, it should mean they were getting higher up, that is to say, they were going in the right direction.

They came to a ridge and as they crossed it, they stood out against the lighter blue of the western sky. A voice shouted in German, "Halt! Stillstehen!"

"Run, run," he cried, dragging her along.

Two shots rang out and then they were back under the rim of the hill and in a field of bushes and rock. "Come on, come on," Michael urged, "hold on."

"I can't," she muttered but he dragged her and then they were amidst high, rocky hills, in almost total darkness. Michael stumbled, he saw a different kind of blackness on the hill in front of him and realized he was facing a cave. He pulled Marie in with him. She very slowly lay down.

He had heard rather than see her do that. "Are you all right?" he asked.

"No."

He kneeled on the ground and moved his hand till he touched her. Her dress was wet. "They got me," she whispered.

A gust of wind from the mouth of the cave hit him. Wet snow began to fall.

Michael, in 1941

15

Nowadays the southern slope of the Sierra Canals is crossed by a turnpike, the auto route to Barcelona. But in the year 1941 it still looked as it had for centuries, a roadless wasteland of rocks and hills, dry heather, bare fields, where only wild animals lived.

A continuity had not yet been broken which went back in time to the defeated Spaniards of the 1930s' republic, to the Carlists, to the guerrilleros attacking the rear guards of Napoleon's armies, and beyond those to the Moors, and to the Carthaginians in the night of a long ago past. A continuity of men who had climbed across those hills to fight or to escape into France from a vengeful enemy.

Michael stood shivering in the mouth of the cave and peered into the distance. He could now make out a fragment of a stone wall, perhaps part of a fortress once guarding the Spanish plain. There was a glimmer of light in the sky, just enough to distinguish the outline of the hills around him.

Behind him he heard Marie moan. He had bound a strip of her black dress around her left thigh where a bullet had gone in, working blindly, and he had wrapped her in his raincoat. She had fallen asleep or perhaps passed out. The snow turned into a slashing rain.

Before dawn the rain stopped. Marie was sleeping now but he could feel she had a fever. If he went out by himself to get help, he would never find the cave back. He had to take her along.

He woke her and to his relief she smiled at him. "We have to get out of here," he said. "You think you can walk leaning on me?"

"I'll try," she whispered. Those were the only words she spoke that day.

The sky had cleared enough to show where the sun was rising, northeast. He took out their last chunk of bread and softened it in a puddle; she shook her head at it. They set out, steering south, she leaning heavily on him. There was no path but in between the outcroppings of rock the ground was quite even, gently sloping downward. Every so often he sat down and she lay with her head in his lap.

They saw stone buildings in the distance but when they got nearer they turned out to be crumbling and abandoned. Once past them though, they came to what looked like traces of an old footpath.

Then, after one more rest, Marie couldn't get up any more.

At that point Michael began to feel despair. No, not despair, disgust comes closer as a word to describe it. He was in a situation he *refused* to accept.

He had offered to help this girl across the border. On a sunny morning, feeling high on the adventure he was in, he had been sitting on a café terrace in France with a nice-looking young woman.

And now it had deteriorated to where he was no longer a free, escaped, soldier. He was like a dreary, anxious husband weighed down by a helpless wife who had got herself shot in the leg. It came completely natural to him that it had been her own clumsiness which had led her to be wounded, and that it could not have happened to him. He would have liked to give up this enterprise now.

But he wasn't for a moment considering to leave her behind, that would not undo his own stupidity of getting into this. It would be out of scale, an evil thing making it all worse.

He emptied his pockets of everything of any weight and put her pocketbook which he had carried, under a rock. Then he lifted her up and started down the path, carrying her in his arms. But he had to stop soon to rest, and putting her down and then lifting her up again reached just the edge of the impossible. He tried carrying her over his shoulder but that made walking hopelessly difficult. During all this she was a load more than a person.

The sun came out and that gave him a push, let's get past that rock, past those bushes, past that patch of nettles. The girl had long lost consciousness, and he saw colors dance before his eyes. He was talking to himself. Another stone building came into view. "It's empty too," he said contemptuously. And then, "It is a fucking ruin all right. Never mind. It still seems to have a roof anyway."

The building was not abandoned. It was standing in a garden of sorts, and he discovered a man in that garden, hoeing or whatever. He struggled on till he reached a stone gate. He stopped, the girl still in his arms, and stared at a name, hard to read, chiselled in the tympanum over the door. "Monasterio de Santa Lucia." He read the name out loud, in a flat voice as if he was looking at it from his seat in a comfortable car. He now started singing, "La, la, la, la, Santa Lu-ciá." Then he collapsed on a patch of dead grass, still holding Marie.

Michel, in 1871 and 1872

16

Michel in his days as a printer, before the Prussians entered Paris, had produced a number of geographical books, and when he started walking south from Vichy in that early summer evening, he had a pretty clear image of the map of France in his mind. The good road south, the one the post coaches followed and where they were now building the railroad, led to Clermont-Ferrand. Clermont was a modern town and it, too, had its share of uprisings and killings after the armistice, though of course nothing on the scale of Paris. And as the Versailles government still appeared interested enough in him to intercept his mail and to send the police after him, he had at all cost to avoid modern France, and reach Spain through old France.

Once across that border, he would be safe to establish proper contact with Anne. She would join him, they could start a new life, in England or even in America. He would write to her about his idea not to be a printer again, to shy away from the wilderness of cities with their veneer of civilization. Would she be willing to be a farmer with him, for wasn't that the only *innocent* life?

He stood still and closed his eyes. It dizzied him, the idea of all the bottlenecks that had to be conquered, just for them to be together again. How could this government of France go on spending so much money and time on finding one man who had not even been a Communard really? How dare they. Who had entrusted them with that power? What if Anne had already given up and was in mourning for him? He tried to conjure up a picture of Anne all in black, but he couldn't, he could only see her in the bright yellow and blue dresses she had worn that spring. That was a good omen, he decided: she had not given up.

At the end of each day he would concentrate all his thought on her, see her, talk to her—who knows but that she would feel it, receive the vibrations? Hadn't that German scientist, Mesmer, proven those things were possible?

The sky kept its promise and it started to rain, but he felt better and struck up a marching tempo. The road signs had been put back up here, or maybe this far from the invading armies they had never been taken down. He would make for Le Puy and then cross the Ardéche, poor, backward country where most people couldn't even read or write and would hardly know there'd been a war; but they were famous for their hospitality. As long as he took care not to sound like a townsman, he'd get a meal for a day's work.

He figured his first night he could spend some money and take a bed at an inn. Then he could dry his clothes and wash and shave. You didn't want to look like a townsman, but not like a tramp either.

But as he trudged on along the dark road, not a sign of human habitation was visible. Finally he had to settle for a night under the trees lining a stream. When he woke up, there was rime on the grass and his throat so painful that he couldn't swallow the water from the stream. After an hour's march in the warm sun he felt better, and his clothes were dry. That day he made it all the way to Ambert, where at a farm they let him sleep in the stable in exchange for him helping clear a field the next day.

A week later he was already way beyond Le Puy and he hadn't spent a franc on food; everywhere he shared the soup with the other laborers. And only once, in a village square where he washed at a horse trough, a gendarme has asked him who he was. But the man had been satisfied with his answer, that he was a prisoner of war of the Prussians, set free, and working his way back to his home in the Ardéche because everything he had ever owned was stolen off him.

It was high summer when he reached Perpignan and blindingly hot. He passed a pharmacy where the thermometer on the wall showed 29 degrees on the scale of Réaumur. He made for the farms to the west of the town and found work for a whole week, earning another ten francs. Two days later he walked from Cerbére out of France and across the border into Spain without a soul bothering him. A douanier at the Spanish side of the border who was smoking his pipe on a kitchen chair in the shade, asked "Traballador ambulante?" and he just nodded. Now he was out of the clutches of Versailles. The postmistress in Perpignan had assured him that the Spanish town of Gerona had one of the new government telegraph offices, and thus Gerona was his goal.

He spent a restless first night in Catalonia. He didn't want to risk sleeping in the open so close to the border, in case some gendarme got the idea that he was a tramp and took him back, so he went to the inn in the border village of La Jonquera. They gave him a plate of beans and let him sleep on the floor near the fire, and he got a lot of Spanish coins in change for the two francs he had put on the counter. But he lay wide awake, staring at the embers and phrasing a message in his mind for Anne. He had never sent or received a telegram but knew you had to leave out every word that wasn't essential. The thought that he would soon speak to her, in a sense, through electricity, was wildly exciting.

Before anyone at the inn had stirred, he was on his way to Gerona, still shaping and reshaping his message. His wariness about his good luck so far, led him to avoid the paved main road, for suppose the inn keeper had been bribed by the French police to report suspicious arrivals? He cut through the fields instead, but before long he got caught in a tremendous thunderstorm. He got hopelessly lost and, cursing his stupidity, tramped for hours under a downpour which turned the ground into mud and completely obliterated his view. Then quite suddenly he found himself in front of a massive building, beautifully decorated with sculpted stone. He went to pull the bell, he was going to ask for directions to the Gerona road or possibly, since it was already getting dark, for a night's shelter.

That decision set Michel on a course of long-lived consequence.

Michel, in 1871

17

THE DOOR WAS OPENED BY A MONK WHO ADDRESSED Michel in Spanish. When he answered, "Francés," he was shown to a large room where a dozen men were eating at a long wooden table, some in monk's robes, others dressed in workman's clothes. He was in the refectory of the monastery; at the head of the table sat a man in a white habit, and Michel was taken over to him.

"I am Brother Gutierre," the monk said in French. "I am the abbot of the house and I welcome you."

"I am Michel Beauchamp," Michel answered, realizing in that same instant, and with pleasure, that he had given his real name and that it was safe to do so. "Excuse me for interrupting your meal. I got lost in the rainstorm."

"You look somewhat the worse for wear, monsieur Beauchamp. Take the chair beside me and eat some soup."

"Thank you," Michel said. "It's some time that I was called monsieur Beauchamp." He sat down.

"If you'll forgive an old man proud of his skills of observance, you have the hands of a poor farm laborer and the face of a city librarian. But please eat your soup."

"I used to be a townsman," Michel answered. "But—"

"But?"

"Let's say, I discovered what our civilized towns are capable of."

"This was in Paris?"

"Yes. Indeed."

"And Paris is often called the capital of our Western civilization. As Rome was once."

Michel shrugged. "It was a citizen of that same Rome who wrote, 'Man is a wolf to man.'"

"And he was being unjust to wolves."

"Precisely."

They smiled at each other.

"Let's go sit by the fire, monsieur Beauchamp. You are dripping wet."

Michel looked at the window behind Gutierre. Black clouds chased across the sky, the day was fading. "You wouldn't want to travel on, would you?" Gutierre asked. "It's not a very propitious night to wander through our hills."

Michel stood up, with hesitation.

"We offer shelter to all travelers,' Gutierre went on. "We charge one peseta a night, but only for those who can afford it."

"I have to hurry to Gerona," Michel answered. "But for tonight, I'd be grateful for shelter."

"Come along then. Bring your bread."

Michel seated himself so close to the fire that his clothes began to steam. "As you can see," Gutierre said, "we are not a medieval monastery. We are poor but we certainly don't believe in hardships for their own sake. They don't help us in our work."

"Which is?"

"We are working priests and working laymen. There is shameful poverty in this province of Spain. We work from within the church, for without such a framework we would be helpless, perhaps in prison. Did you know that Spain is in as much turmoil right now as Paris was after the German victory?"

"You know about that, mister, I mean, Brother Gutierre?"

"Just call me Gutierre. You are not a Catholic, I would guess."

"Well—I was as a child. But—"

"But you don't believe in the love of God," Gutierre said.

"Do you?"

"Sometimes. When I am happy."

"I was a printer," Michel said. "I printed classical texts, and then I printed the plans of the Paris Commune. Here you had men, and women too, who after surviving one more siege, one more war, thought that a new beginning could be made. Had to be made. They were wrong, they called up such hatred, and felt so much hatred in return—the citizens of the capital of Western civilization began slaughtering each other like—I can't think of a parallel. I've seen soldiers shoot a child that came running out of a burning house. I, and my wife Anne— That is why I have to hurry to Gerona, to send her a telegram. We lost contact."

"Gerona has a telegraph bureau."

"Yes."

A silence.

"But we cannot give up on our duty to try and make this earth a better place," Gutierre said.

"Oh but we can. I can. All we can do within our own life is not to hurt people."

"That is a skimpy plan for filling a man's life on earth."

"Perhaps, but you see, different from you and from these men here, I have no desire any more to convert anyone. Those duties you talk about are prescriptions for arrogance and then for cruelty and bloodshed. We haven't got it in us to make a happy world."

"Don't forget, Beauchamp, that even the most overbearing men and the vilest tyrants are in the end pathetic creatures, afraid of eternity."

After a while Gutierre told him, "Two years ago, almost three now, our queen was forced into exile. That was a good thing. That *raza falsa* as we say, that spurious race of the Bourbon kings and queens, finally left the stage. Now, like in France, men here try making a republic. 'Volunteers of Liberty' they call themselves. While in the hills around us the Carlists are assembling to put yet another king on the throne, 'for Jesus' as they say. And in the meantime republican guerrilleros are burning down the churches."

"And you?"

"We just go on quietly, trying to protect the peasants from all of these. Showing them how to grow better crops."

"And they leave you alone?"

"Well—we have heard that a certain group of guerrilleros was focusing on this monastery but the threat may blow over. We certainly have our enemies, if for mistaken reasons."

At sunrise Michel was on his way to Gerona. The abbot had refused his peseta for the night and he had accompanied Michel for the first mile, to make sure he took the right path. They hugged each other when they said farewell. Those two men had found a sympathy of ideas in each other.

Michel had been warned it was a ten-hour hike to the town, but he did it in eight, taking his rest at midday only to eat the bread they had given him at the monastery. He came to the telegraph office in Gerona just as an elderly woman was locking its door.

He ran. "Señora," he shouted, "please! It's a matter of life and death!"

"Young man, the telegraph is open day and night. We are in the nineteenth century here in Gerona. But I was going to eat my little supper. However, we will send your telegram first." She unlocked the door and turned up the lamp. "Where is it going to?"

"Paris, madam," Michel said, suddenly worried about the accuracy of the statement by the post office woman in Perpignan.

"I'm not certain the line is restored. But don't worry, it will definitely go as far as Versailles and then they'd send the international telegrams to Paris by courier."

"Madame Anne Beauchamp, 17 Rue Ramponeau, Paris 20th arr. All is well. Send word. All my love." She looked at Michel with a half-smile. "It does need a signature," she said, "That's in our rulebook. And an address to send the answer to. Or does Madame Anne know? Sit down, young man, don't rush so. My supper will wait for this. Happily."

"Can I give this office as my address?"

"You write, 'Poste Restante, Gerona, Spain.' There is a one peseta charge for that. Plus the charge for the four words of course. Never mind the commas. But what about your name?"

Michel hesitated. "I am Michel Beauchamp. But I—I have reasons not to give my name, it could make the telegram not go through."

"Do not worry, Michel, I think I understand. My late husband escaped from Paris in 1848 after another Glorious Week—not very glorious for him. But that's why you find me still remembering my French, such as it is."

"Your French is beautiful, madam."

"Thank you. How are we going to sign this message, that is the question."

"Can I sign, 'Brother Gutierre, Monastery Santa Lucia?'"

"But you are not this Brother."

"No, but that's my address."

"Let's just sign Monastery Santa Lucia, Poste Restante Gerona. I think that will satisfy the rules."

"I thank you very much. May I ask your name?"

"I am Madame Labouchière Sotelo, a sus ordenes."

"How long will an answer take, madam?"

"A day. Twelve hours if we are lucky. Isn't it astonishing?"

MICHEL FOUND A BAR where they let him sleep in the courtyard for twenty-five centimos and he was back at the telegraph office as the town was waking up. The woman was already there and shook her head before he had asked anything. "Not yet. But the international telegrams usually come in one bundle from the wire station, around ten. Go sit in the café across the street, Michel. I'll wave at you from the door when your answer comes."

At twelve noon, when the bells of Gerona were ringing the hour and the shopkeepers were taking in their wares and locking up for their siesta, she came to stand in the doorway and waved at him, but in an oddly defeated way. Michel walked slowly across the street. "What is it?" he asked in a trembling voice.

She handed him a sealed envelope with the printed words, "Mensaje de Administración." "It looks like some kind of problem, Michel."

The sun was just climbing above the houses on the other side of the road. Michel looked at it and a sense of doom came over him. I won't open this until the sun is free of the roofs, he thought. He stood motionless while the woman stared at him. He opened the envelope.

On a strip of paper inside was written in a clerk's neat hand, in French, "Undeliverable. Addressee (mme) Beauchamp, Paris, deceased."

A black curtain descended on Michel's world. The telegraph woman made him drink a jar of rum which he threw up in the gutter. He wandered out into the town and went through a time of sitting in the street, leaning against the walls of the houses, while occasionally a passer-by would toss a coin in his lap. The sight of a man at the end of his tether has not been unusual in the streets of Spain during most of its history.

After three days of this he left Gerona on the road back to the monastery. It took him twenty-four hours this time for he stopped and turned back to Gerona a number of times, telling himself he had misread the message, he should have insisted on confirmation, tried again. When he finally reached the Santa Lucia he had the appearance of a ghost. The monk who opened the door for him took him without a word to the abbot.

He sat facing Gutierre, unable to speak, let alone to explain his return. Finally he stammered, "Please don't say it was the will of God or any of that kind of idea."

"I would never say such things, Michel. In all the world only man is capable of willing evil." And then he added, "You did well to come back here."

Michel had put the strip of paper in Gutierre's hand. He took it back and tore it up into small pieces.

Michel, in 1871

18

That same night Michel woke up when the bells of the monastery started ringing. Midnight mass, he thought for one moment. He got up from his straw mattress and opened the door of his cell (he had slept with his clothes on, it was very cold in there). Day was breaking, he heard shouts and saw men running around. He grabbed a monk's arm. "Frater Gutierre, por favor!" The man shook himself loose and ran into the courtyard. Gutierre was standing there arguing in a circle of monks. When he saw Michel, he called him over.

"Beauchamp. Yes, trouble. Sooner than expected. But there's time. Leave quickly, follow the path you came in on today, going west, you'll see the moon setting. If you're challenged, only say 'Francès,' nothing else. They'll leave you alone."

Michel stood staring at him.

"Go, man."

"I'd rather stay."

Gutierre seemed about to protest but then he just rested his hand for a moment on Michel's shoulder.

Later Michel was posted at one of the two little windows beside the front entrance, and they gave him a rifle. It made him laugh in spite of himself, it was a muzzle loader heavily decorated with arabesques. It didn't matter, he wasn't going to shoot at anybody. Presently guerrilleros became visible, they were taking cover behind the trees and the garden wall, and not too carefully. Clearly they didn't take the monks very seriously as opponents.

A man approached the house, he was in what Michel assumed a Spanish army officer's uniform, and he waved a white handkerchief. He stopped some twenty feet from the house and delivered a message in a loud voice. Then he walked away.

Michel sought out Gutierre. "He called on us to surrender, what else," Gutierre said. "If we do, he told us, we can walk away and they'll burn the buildings down. If we don't, they'll burn them down and shoot us. They're the 'Volunteers of Liberty.'"

Michel looked around at the monks. Their heated discussions had come to an end, they were strangely silent. "And?" he asked.

"We can't. There are good reasons to think they'd shoot us anyway."

"There seem to be a lot of them," Michel said, "and their rifles are not from the curio shop, like ours."

A volley of shots went off outside and they heard the breaking of glass and a muffled scream. "Take proper cover!" Gutierre shouted at the men "And don't waste ammunition."

"What did you tell 'em?" Michel asked but Gutierre didn't answer. Michel put his rifle on the floor. "Gutierre, I want to talk to them. Let us go out front. I want to talk to them and you must translate."

"You think a Parisian will scare them off?"

"No. Please. Give me a chance."

Gutierre looked hard at him and then shook his head. "No.

You stay out of this. You have your own burden. Climb out at the back and take the path I told you about."

Michel walked to the front door, undid the two heavy bolts, and stepped out into the garden. He waved his handkerchief which was dirty but still recognizably white.

"Compañeros republicanos!" he cried.

A single shot rang out. He felt it hit his thigh, a pain as of a lash with an iron whip. But he didn't cry out and he didn't move. If I do, all is lost, he thought, if I fall, there will be a massacre here. Behind him Gutierre had come out of the building and tried to pull him back.

"Compañeros republicanos!" Michel cried again. And said to Gutierre, "Translate! Please!"

Gutierre hesitated.

"Compañeros, I am a Communard from Paris. I fled to Spain! And this monastery gave me shelter."

"Translate," he said again, and now Gutierre repeated his words in Catalan, "We share your belief in the Republic!"

Several men facing him had stepped away from behind their coverage and stood there openly looking at him.

Michel faltered but then went on and in his loud voice, "I understand your feelings about the parasitical priests who suck the peasants dry! But this, this monastery, is the wrong place. Here live *thin* monks. They are the only support of the poor in this province. Monks who are working men. Monks who are thin."

For "thin" he had used the French word "mince" which Gutierre translated as if he had said "frail." One of the men watching them laughed, and Michel thought, I got them.

"I bring you the republican greetings from Paris," he shouted. "There we have lost the battle, but the war is never lost." There was excitement noticeable now among the 'Volunteers' who started talking among themselves.

"We can only win as brothers," Michel cried. "If we fight among ourselves, if men of good will in this world shoot at each other, the men of ill will must always win. There is too much sadness in the world. Let us not add to it here. We—" His voice broke and he could not go on.

But after those words had been heard in Catalan, the officer who had earlier delivered the ultimatum, came out from behind the garden wall. He walked up to Michel and embraced him.

Now everywhere the attackers came out from behind their cover and monks streamed out of the building. Men embraced each other. In the hubbub Gutierre took Michel's hand and said, "You saved the day." Michel smiled at him, and fell over.

"Dear God," Gutierre cried, "the man was standing in a pool of blood."

They carried him inside and cut away his clothing. They bandaged his wound and took him to the one room in the monastery which had a real bed. It belonged to an Andalusian botanist, known as the Sybarite. He often stayed there, he was working on the local crop diseases.

The monks took turns nursing Michel but his fever wouldn't abate and finally they sent for the doctor in Figueras who came and took the bullet out.

On the first day Michel's head was clear, Gutierre quickly came and sat by his bedside. "Monsieur Beauchamp," he began, "we are without words—"

"I'm so glad to hear that," Michel murmured and closed his eyes again.

Gutierre was taken aback but it didn't silence him for long.

"Beauchamp, Michel, Miguel well-named after the Archangel, you will stay here until you have all your old strength back. And, I hope personally, thereafter. We have a very fine library."

MICHEL, IN 1871

19

THREE MONTHS LATER A PREMATURE WINTER WAS ALready descending on those foothills of the Pyrenees. The sparse oak trees had lost their leaves, wet snow and sleet came down at all hours. Only the refectory had a fire but Michel spent most of his waking hours in the library where he could as a rule be on his own, but where his hands and feet turned raw and itching with the penetrating cold.

He welcomed those miseries distracting him, he read through the library books (those in French and Latin) at great speed. But Anne and their unborn son or daughter kept pushing out other thought.

At times he asked himself furiously, I didn't really love her all that much, did I? Or if I did, it could not have stayed that way, not in daily life—pure love should not become such a desperate obsession. Pure love, what does it consist of? Perhaps it is, as they now tell us, simply a magnetic imbalance, a chemical reaction. Yes, my sweet Anne, I long for you simply the way a sodium atom longs for a chlorine atom. He conjured up her face, how she would look if he had told her that, surprised, hurt, and then laughing, and tears came to his eyes.

Perhaps now his love for Anne was in part pity, the immense pity he felt as he imagined her death, caught in a firefight, or in a burning house, or, worst of all possibilities, by her execution as the wife of an escaped Communard. He sat under the round library window, holding his book up to the light of day. He hated lighting a lamp and using up resources of the monastery, for he was staying for free now. He had no more money and Gutierre did not want him to pay anyway.

One day he had come to fetch him in the library. "I have something to show you, Miguel."

He led Michel to the corridor off the main entrance, and there a tile had been embedded in the stone wall, with a text in Latin. "Deo Gratias," it proclaimed, "Anno Domini MDCCCLXXI the Monastery of Santa Lucia and its inhabitants were saved from death and destruction, by the sacrificial courage of a layman guest, our brother Michel Beauchamp, Paris printer and exile."

Greatly embarrassed, Michel had fled back to the library. They don't know, he thought, that I made that speech without any warmth either for them or for their cause, I could do it, bleeding like a pig as I was, because I didn't give a damn any more about anything. It felt like being a person in a history book, that Roman who put his hand in the fire, or the boy in Sparta with the fox under his jacket. It was a scene from a long-ago era, something you'd find in Paris only in the theater.

Meanwhile he read through the odes of Horace. Exegi monumentum aere perennius, I have erected a monument more durable than bronze. But everyone who has ever existed should have their monument more durable than bronze. Otherwise, where is justice?

One day at sunset Gutierre came to visit him and they looked over the ragged fields. "Ten acres won't feed one family there," Gutierre remarked.

"But it's very picturesque."

"Yes. Picturesque."

"We have a guest at our table tonight," Gutierre said. "Please talk to him. He is from Figueras, our near-neighbor town. No more than an hour's walk from here."

"I've seen it," Michel answered. "Last month, the last warm days, I've wandered around there. It's a miserable little town. Why do I have to talk to a man from there?"

"He is a printer. He needs a workshop manager, a foreman."

"A foreman," Michel repeated.

"We are concerned, Miguel. You have to take up your profession, you have to renew your life. If you were one of us, we'd pray with you. But you are a worldly man and you have to find your salvation in this world first. You have to work."

"Horace is work," Michel said, holding up his book.

"Take the job in Figueras," Gutierre asked. "I told the man you have Latin and that is all he had to hear. It's an hour's walk. At the end of the day you and I will eat our soup together and consider life—unless you or I want to be left alone. When you are healed, as you will be one day, you will stay with us and study or be our librarian, or you will go back into the world. Some future government in France will decree an amnesty and you may want to go back and be a Paris printer again. And you will always have a home here."

"I, I will never pardon them," Michel answered and they stayed silent a long time.

"Brother Gutierre," Michel said at last, "Perhaps you should know that I was happy, when we were attacked. I had just learned of Anne's death. I wish I had been killed that day. And all I said to those Liberty Volunteers was pure sophism. The only words that came from, from within myself, were, 'there is too much sadness in the world.' So much for owing me gratitude."

"There's no fate linking your Anne's death to your saving the Santa Lucia," Gutierre answered. "Read Juvenal next, 'It's us humans who have made fate a goddess. She isn't.' The only link between them is in you. You are a good man whether you like it or not."

"Sacra simplicitas," Michel muttered.

"I had a son once and you remind me of him. Maybe that moves me more strongly even than what you call undeserved gratitude."

"What happened to him?"

"He was killed during the coup d'état of General O'Donnell. He was on the Calle Mayor in Madrid that day in 1841, with the students of the university. They were taking turns reading out texts from such criminals as Plato and Erasmus— He was killed in a fusillade, from our glorious army."

MICHEL TOOK the print job in Figueras. At the hour when the monks went to the first mass, he set out along the narrow road which led to the Spanish tableland; by eight in the morning he was at the workshop. Gutierre had made out a pass for him, a laissez-passer giving his name as Brother Miguel and the monastery as his place of residence, and with no nationality filled in. Mother Church will be your nation for a while, Gutierre had said.

As in Vichy, Michel kept to himself there. He soon mastered enough Spanish to do his job well. At six in the evening he started back to the monastery and had Gutierre to talk to, while they had their soup. He was paid a hundred and fifty pesetas a month which he put in a box as the monks continued to refuse his money. On Sundays he worked on the neglected library catalogue. The long hike to Figueras and back restored his strength, but he continued to live in a kind of fog he only broke through in the middle of the night, lying awake and thinking of what could have been. Being back in his old profession left him unmoved. I was right, it has lost its innocence, he thought.

It was early in the new year, still close to the solstice, that on a cold but calm day the sky turned black at noon and a fierce winter storm broke. By early afternoon the men got worried; the wind was steadily gaining in strength and the snow came down in a blizzard. It was decided to close up shop early and one of them offered to put up Michel for the night. He declined, he knew the road to the monastery by heart now.

It was worse than he had imagined. At one time, perhaps halfway, he thought that he very well might not make it. The howling wind from the north hit him as if it were a live force determined to bring him to a stop. The snow froze in his eyebrows and he had to keep rubbing his face to see anything of the road ahead.

It was then that the idea passed through his mind how painless it would be to just lie down and finish a life he did not expect much of any more. But no sooner had the thought come up that he heard himself say, "Anne is alive. And our child is alive." The words came as a violent shock, as if not out of his own mouth but out of the dark and they immediately and unquestionably appeared true. Tears of happiness started running down his face, he went on twice as fast, and was back at the monastery without remembering anything of the second half of his journey.

Before dawn, without saying a word to anyone, he took all

his money from the box, his few possessions, and his church pass, and walked back to Figueras. The snow had stopped and the high wind, now in his back, hurried him on. Two hours later he was on the local train to Perpignan and onward to Paris.

Michel, in 1872

20

All during that journey to Paris Michel was in a fever. He sat upright in his third-class seat and the train conductors got used to see him furiously pace up and down the platform at each stop, while his fellow travelers lined up at the railroad bar.

When he came out of the station and was actually standing in a Paris street, he was dizzy from the apprehensions and premonitions parading through his mind. He forced himself to enter a café and drink a glass of beer and eat some rolls. Then he boarded the horse omnibus to Ménilmontant.

The streets were crowded, the civil war damage seemed to have disappeared. But he did not look out for long, he closed his eyes and tried to stop all thought. It was early evening when he knocked on the door of his apartment at 17, Rue Ramponeau. Silence. Oh my God, let her be there. Let her be.

Steps. The door opened. For one instant he saw Anne in the person who opened the door, he tried to shout her name. Then he saw it was a man. It was his former neighbor, Henri Labin the ivory trader. Michel's mouth formed words, but not a sound came out.

"Monsieur Beauchamp," Labin said slowly. "What an enormous surprise."

They looked at each other.

"But come in," Labin said. "Come in for a moment."

Michel took two hesitant steps and stood in the dark corridor. "Here, come in the kitchen," Labin said. "You know the way. I was making coffee."

Michel sat down. He did not dare ask the one question.

"The water will boil soon," Labin announced. He seemed stunned too. Then he went on, "Your lease had lapsed, you know. The owner offered this apartment to me, and there seemed to be no reason not to take it, I always knew it was much better than my old place. Of course if I had known—" he didn't finish that sentence. "The ivory trade is picking up again. It's surprising how quickly things have returned to normal. Well, that is to say—our losses of course, I mean the loss of so many, your loss, that is something else, of course. I tend you my condolences, Beauchamp."

"My—"

"I mean, for the loss of your wife."

"Anne is dead?" Michel asked in so low a voice that Labin had to guess what he was asking.

"Didn't you—I mean—"

"Is her death a certainty?" Michel heard himself ask.

"I—well, yes. Sadly so. The police came, they said they didn't know what had become of you— I assume you have been pardoned now? I told them you had been a professional printer who didn't have to share the opinions of your customers, how absurd! But as you were both, eh, deceased, they were taking your possessions and, eh, effects, just in safekeeping, mind you, until the courts decide—" Labin had been told that Michel had been shot while trying to escape, but he left that out. He was standing in the kitchen, holding out to Michel a ridiculous cup of coffee. "They took everything?" Michel whispered, stepping back into the dark corridor.

"The only thing they forgot was her picture, the drawing that used to hang in your workroom."

"Where is it now?"

Labin walked past him and entered another room. He came back with a parcel. "I wrapped it up, I was waiting to see—"

Michel left without another word, with the picture under his arm. He walked all the way back to the South station and got on the night train back to Perpignan. He took the picture out of its frame and put it under his shirt.

The train was half empty and he spread newspaper out on the floor of his compartment and lay down. In Lyon he had to change trains. It was evening once more when his train had come to Cerbère, the border station with Spain. During the twenty-four hours of the journey Michel had not had one clear thought. He had a fever and the others passengers gave him a wide berth as he was talking to himself.

On the way up, the control in Cerbère had been nominal and his church pass had not been questioned. Now everyone had to get out to go through the controls, and when Michel presented his church laisser-passer he was asked to step into the office.

"Are you Michel Beauchamp?" he was asked, and when he nodded, he was told he was under arrest as a fugitive from justice.

MICHEL, IN 1872

21

WHEN MICHEL WAS TAKEN FROM HIS CELL TO THE courtroom, he and the policeman guarding him passed through a waiting room crowded with lawyers and prisoners. He caught sight of himself in a fly-specked mirror which (for no conceivable reason) hung there and he stopped. I wouldn't have recognized myself in the street, he thought. He had spent several months waiting for his court appearance, in an unheated cell of six by six feet in the Perpignan jail. His face had the color of ashes, his lips were covered with scabs, and the barber, a fellow prisoner, who had shaved him that morning, had cut him in a number of places. "Yes, you're a beauty," the policeman said, pushing him on.

When he shuffled in front of the judge in his shoes without laces, he thought he could read the contempt on the faces of the judge and his assessor. (Actually, their thoughts were elsewhere, and Michel didn't look any worse than the dozen or so men and woman who had already that morning been dragged before them and dragged away again.)

"Beauchamp," the judge said. "You were put under a death sentence on the 29th of May of last year in Paris, you escaped, and you were caught traveling on false church papers, clearly pretending to be a religious man rather than an atheist. Do you have anything to say before I order the death sentence to be carried out?"

He did not even look at Michel while speaking those words, he was reading a document, a pen ready in his right hand.

He is all set to cross out my life, Michel thought, without so much as giving me a look. The bastard. "Yes, indeed!" he cried out in a thick voice. He was copying the booming tones of the school chaplain from his Collège Chaptal days which he remembered so well. "Now I know it says in the Book of St. John, 'Judge not by appearance,' but we are not told that means a man should be condemned without so much as looking at him."

Now both the judge and the assessor were staring at him.

"In Paris I was not accused of anything," Michel went on, "much less tried. The papers I am traveling with are not false. I am not an atheist but an agnostic. For all you know, sir, I am a more religious man than you."

The judge bent over to the assessor and whispered with him, while the assessor searched through his papers, apparently in vain.

"This hearing is adjourned for ten days," the judge said. "The prisoner will remain held in close confinement."

WHEN MICHEL REAPPEARED before the judge, the man looked hard at him. Since his court had been in session, the judge had dealt with dozens of prisoners, sent many to prison, and some to their deaths; but Michel had been the only man he really saw.

"There is no transcript or other record of any Paris proceedings," the judge said." The fact remains, prisoner, that you were a Communard. I sentence you to ten years of hard labor."

Michel closed his eyes, there was a roar in his head.

"However," the judge continued, "I am giving you a chance to repay your debt to France. If you enlist this day in the Régiments Etrangers, and for a minimum period of ten years, I will make the prison sentence probationary."

Michel stared at him.

"Well?" the judge asked impatiently. His moment of empathy with Michel was over. "What is your choice, man?"

"The Régiments, Judge. The Régiments."

"What *are* the Regiments Etrangers?" Michel asked the guard who took him back to his cell. Until then no one had talked to him, but now he was looked at differently.

"It's what the public calls the Foreign Legion," the guard said with a grin. "I don't envy you, fellow. Their noncoms make us prison guards look like Sisters of Charity." Michel wasn't the least unnerved by this reply. He did not care.

That same evening Michel was put in handcuffs and taken over to the lock-up of the Perpignan military barracks, where he had to sign his enlistment papers, and was given a bowl of soup made from fish heads, a chunk of dark bread, and (a good omen, he felt) a cup of red wine. Two days later he was in the hold of a packet boat, with a dozen fellow prisoners, on his way to Algeria (which by then had already been a French colony for forty years).

Michel, in 1872

22

The packet made its landfall in Bône and that morning, in the barracks of the Legion, prisoners and volunteers were lined up together for their first roll call, followed by cold showers, shaving of heads, and delousing. Then the men stood in line, naked, for a uniform, sand-colored underwear, socks, a short heavy coat, and leather boots which felt like iron and were called cockroach killers.

The dormitory Michel was assigned to had twelve double-deck bunks with a three-foot locker for each man. Every bunk had a straw mattress, a pillow, and a horse blanket. The latrine was in the corridor and consisted of two pilgrim toilets, that is to say, holes in the ground. Outside was a cold-water tap and a bucket. You wiped yourself with your hand, a corporal explained, then you washed your hand under the tap, and used the bucket for flushing. He said it slowly, and twice, for many of the men weren't French. Michel heard German and English, and languages he couldn't identify.

But the windows of the dormitory were open at the top and a warm breeze blew through. I've had much worse, Michel thought, and for the first time since he had faced Labin in his Paris apartment, he felt some strength within himself. This won't be so tough. And what's more, they cannot stop me from escaping. Bône is not far from the border of Tunisia.

MICHEL HAD SOME LUCK, finally. The sergeant of his company was not one of those sadistic Legion noncoms he had now heard so much about. This sergeant was an old soldier who above all cherished "a quiet life," as he repeatedly told his men. Michel was put in the company office by him and he didn't even bother to send him on the marches and weapon exercises. "I've got enough men who can kill an Arab," he told Michel. "What I want from you is, my administration in order. That's what I want from you. Just salute the officers according to the book and no one will be any the wiser."

It was an odd life that thus began for Michel. Up at 4:30 in the morning, roll-call, bread and black coffee, six hours in the office shifting papers, trying to balance the company account, copying out orders and receipts, and making lists of men who had died, were being punished, sent to the military hospital in Constantine, invalided out or discharged (with a cheap suit and a steerage ticket to Marseilles). Soup with half a liter of red wine, followed by more office. An evening meal of stew and another half liter. On Sundays, a glass of cognac.

He shared the office with one other man, a haggard veteran of countless battles with a gray beard and a narrow breast covered with campaign ribbons, who rarely spoke a word. One day this man dropped his pen, fell out of his chair, and silently died. He was never replaced because Michel could easily do all the work.

In the evening Michel walked through the little streets of the suburb where the barracks stood. The numerous cafés and bars were out of bounds to the new recruits, the *bleus* as they were called, and in the one coffee house where they were allowed, they were the only customers.

Summer was over. The smell of the wood fires hid the daytime stink of the hot sun on the shit and the rotting food in the gutters. Aged whores with sores on their faces stood around trying to tempt the bleus. The chumminess among the recruits, interspersed with fist fights and fights with bottles and knives, passed him by. He was left alone, and maybe even liked, for he was always ready to help someone who was in trouble with the army bureaucracy.

He endlessly reexamined his past, his becoming a printer because of his Latin and his kinship with a vanished world of the classic poets and adventurers of Greece and Rome which—as he knew himself—was more imagined than real. But the death of Anne remained the whirlpool in which any ideas he had about the future vanished.

On bad nights he took the portrait of her out of his locker. He had lost it at his arrest but when he was transferred to the Legion barracks they had given it back to him, together with his wallet containing some fifty pesetas, and a pouch of dried-out tobacco. He'd light a candle he had stolen from the mess room and stare at her, sitting up in his bunk. Sometimes a thought stirred in him that one day he would really live again, work again, and that the portrait would hang in his room and that he would be able to look at it with a warm melancholy. But then he would think that if that were to happen it would be a tragedy also, a second death for her.

Wet snow was falling on the Legion post, "very early, very rare," everyone agreed. He felt it fitted the grayness of the cavernous buildings better than that eternally steel-blue sky of summer. It fitted the institutional green of the walls, the color of the dead grass, and the color of the *purpose* of it all, of which he only got to see the abstract: the names of the Legionnaires who had died of wounds or, more often, disease, their hospital stays, amputations, funerals, and discharges, and the numbers (no names) of the dead Arabs on the other side.

The time had come to make his escape. If they had treated him the way he had expected, with harassments and blows, he would have fled long ago, or been killed, but the low-key sergeant and the silent office made it all too easy to sink in a routine of day following day, all alike.

But contrary to what that Perpignan judge seemed to think, he said to himself, I owe no debt to my country. It owes me a debt which can never be repaid. And yet here I am, shuffling papers, being in my own small way its accomplice. Ten years. Imagine it.

On that first day when the recruits had gotten their uniforms and become bleus, they had been told that no Legionnaire had ever deserted and lived. "The Legion is now your father and mother," an officer had told them at assembly. "But a deserter is a renegade. The Legion always finds a renegade and knows how to deal with him."

Tunis, Michel thought. We aren't more than sixty kilometers from the border. Tunisia's definitely still an independent country with its own king or sheik or whatever he is called. If I can get away at night, it won't be noticed until 4:30 in the morning. That gives me six hours. I need to carry water and some food. And I need clothes, European ones, but shabby. No masquerades. I'll be a poor-white settler. But I need a compass. I need to buy a compass in Bône without raising suspicion. I have to get downtown for that, and during the day. I could write a purchase order on Legion paper and say I am sent by the lieutenant. Above all, I need more money, French money.

He could think of little else now but his escape. He'd break into a cold sweat at the thought of how easily it could go wrong.

Should I try to steal money from the cash box in the paymaster's office? Old European clothes—what happened to the stuff we came in? It must be stored somewhere. And that damn compass.

Now it was torture to see the hours and the days go by, and he became afraid of himself, he was certain that he'd come to the point where he would just make off, without compass, without anything, and get caught miserably, and get shot as they had wanted to for so long now anyway.

But there was another outcome in store for him.

HE SAT at his wobbly table looking at the casualty lists which had been brought in from the Touggourt desert post. He wondered if his sergeant's remark, that there had been no casualties there in recent months, signified that the sergeant hadn't been informed yet, or if it was meant as a hint to him that he had to lose those figures when he drew up the report.

He was stirring up the muddy liquid in his inkwell when he heard a rifle shot. It startled him and made him knock over the ink.

He got up to search for a piece of blotting paper and as he passed the door to the courtyard, he stepped out to look. A very young man, a boy really, in an Arab djelaba, ran past him pursued by the guard of the main gate. The Legionnaire kneeled on one knee and fired his rifle at the boy, but he missed and the bullet shattered Michel's right elbow.

A month later Michel was dismissed from the hospital in Constantine and brought back to the Legion post in Bône.

"I feel sorry about your arm, my friend," the old sergeant said. Michel's arm had been amputated above the elbow. "The lieutenant wants to see you about your discharge from the Legion." (It would be the first and only time that an officer would speak with him). "I put in my report," the sergeant added, "that you were wounded in a gun fight with an Arab anarchist who had penetrated into the Legion grounds. Well, that is the truth, isn't it?"

"Thank you, sergeant."

"It'll help, you know. And it lets Jacquot off the hook. He is not much of a marksman, never has been."

THE LIEUTENANT told Michel, "At ease." And went on, "Your position is complex, Beauchamp. Irregular."

Michel remained silent, as the sergeant had told him to.

"I see in your file that you signed up for ten years by court order. Now if you had been killed outright, it would have been simple."

"I'm sorry, sir," Michel said.

The lieutenant gave him a sharp look but decided that a man with such a bland face couldn't have tried to be ironic. "I'm not sure of the precedents," he said. "Of course we can't use a man with one arm, but we can't discharge you either, not with our hands tied by that court order. I think I'll let them figure it out in France."

"You mean I have to go back to France, sir?"

"Well, man, where else would you go? There aren't all that many jobs for a cripple. And you're not legally free anyway. In

France you might even qualify for a Legion disability pension, think of that."

"Sir?"

"Disability—that means you're disabled. It's modest, the Legion is the poor relative in our army. For one arm, it's twenty-five francs a month. Still, you're a young man, you'll have cost us a lot of money in the end."

A man had knocked and came into the office. "Corporal. Escort this man to the barracks, help him assemble his belongings. Then you'll take him to the Marseilles evening packet. Tell their sergeant-at-arms to keep an eye on him."

"In Marseilles you report to the Legion post," he told Michel. "The sergeant-at-arms will take you there. Here are your papers, don't lose them. You can collect the pay due to you here, before you leave, that way you can buy a glass of wine and a bite to eat on the ship. Well, good luck, Beauchamp. Dismissed."

The corporal said, "Permission to ask a question, sir."

"Granted."

"Does he travel in handcuffs, sir?"

The lieutenant thought this over. "Handcuff his left arm to your arm, you mean? I think not. We're not going to handcuff a one-armed veteran. Not the Legion, corporal."

Michel had to sign various papers (he had already taught himself to write with his left hand). He was given back his old trousers, the jacket they had given him in the monastery, a coupon for a steerage passage on the packet boat, and thirty-two francs back pay (after deductions).

When he stood with the corporal at the gang plank of the ship in the early evening, waiting for the sergeant-at-arms to make an appearance, he said, "Here, corp, go drink my health somewhere," and gave him ten francs. "You don't have to wait, I'm not going anywhere."

"All right, Beauchamp. Good luck to you." The corporal was about to shake hands but thought better of it. Michel saluted him and went aboard.

It was dark when the crew got ready to cast off and when Michel jumped back on the quay and vanished amidst the spectators waiting for the ship to leave. In the old town a street vendor gave him ten francs for his boat ticket, and at the waterfront he soon found a coastal brig being loaded for Tunis, and his remaining francs bought him a deck passage.

Just before dawn he was standing on the pier of Goletta, the harbor of Tunis, capital of Tunisia, still an independent nation though formally under Turkish suzerainty.

Michael, in 1941

23

When Michael opened his eyes, he looked at a ceiling of rough beams and planks, all blackened with age. He was lying on a straw mattress in what must be a monk's cell, in his raincoat and soaked shoes. The wall had a square opening which showed ink-black clouds, and a freezing wind blew in. They just dumped me here, he thought. Not very promising. He painfully got up and opened the door. A stone corridor and across from him another door. He looked in and saw a very large room with book shelves everywhere but with no trace of books.

Here they had proper windows with glass in them. A man was sitting near one, studying a document, and Michael went over to him. "Excuse me," he said, "Do you speak English or French?"

The man sighed and beckoned Michael to follow him. In the corridor he pointed to another door and then returned to his bookless library.

Michael knocked and entered a small office. A man in a white monk's habit was sitting at a desk and stood up when Michael came in. "I am glad to see you back on your feet," he said in a strongly accented English and without looking very glad. "I am the abbot of this monastery."

"I am sorry. I guess I passed out more or less. We had a bad time. I'm okay now, but the girl, she was wounded, was there someone to take care of her? How is she?"

The abbot frowned. "The woman is in a hut. I put a blanket over her. That is all I can do. Women may not enter the monastery, on no account."

"But she has been shot! She has a high fever!"

"I cannot help her. The wound is in the upper leg. We cannot look at a woman's body. Touch it, never."

Michael turned pale. "Of all the asshole—why didn't you wake me, sir?"

"We tried."

"A woman is bleeding—to death, possibly. Does that sound like sexual temptation to you?"

"You tell me she is shot," the abbot answered angrily. "By who? A frontier guard? That will put our order at risk."

"Please, can I see her?"

The monk got up and walked out of the room, Michael following him. They went out the front door and the man pointed at a shed. "In there."

"Could you please have someone bring me water and bandages? Or just clean linen?"

The man walked away and Michael ran to the shed. Marie was lying on a cot, covered with a blanket. She was in a feverish sleep, muttering. He lifted the blanket, her dress was coated with blood and it stuck to her skin, but the bleeding appeared to have stopped. He heard steps and hastily opened the door of the shed; a man was walking away and did not turn his head. He had put a jug with a towel on top of it on the ground near the door.

Dabbing it with water, Michael managed to loosen Marie's

dress from her skin. The wound looked ugly and swollen. He soaked the towel and tied it around it; she groaned but her eyes remained closed.

Michael hurried back to the office of the abbot. Another monk was sitting there, in black, who gave him a friendly smile. 'I'm grateful for your shelter," Michael said. "I am sorry if I was rude, I am very worried. Can you send for a doctor? I am an American, our consul will pay the expense."

The man had listened attentively but then answered, "No entiendo." He pointed to the other chair. "Please."

Time passed. Michael kept jumping up and then the monk would wave him back to his chair, point at a clock, make a calming gesture. At last the abbot came back.

Michael stood up, began, "I must ask you—" The abbot held up a hand. "You can both stay till tomorrow. Not longer. We cannot shelter a woman. We cannot shelter refugees from the police. This is a severe state, our new Spain. You put our monastery in danger."

Michael fell back into his chair. An immense weariness took hold of him again. How could I have miscalculated so? These guys are fascists, well, we knew that, didn't we. The bastards. Wait till this war is over. He said, "Can you let me have aspirins, just aspirins? Do you have iodine? And please get a doctor today and let him decide. I am an American, our consulate in Madrid will reimburse you. And in dollars. Please send for a doctor."

The abbot stared at him, sneeringly, Michael thought. The abbot said, "The only doctor in our area is the army doctor in Figueras. If he comes here and sees a shot wound, he brings the Guardia Civil and we all go to prison. And the woman and you may be shot. Do not talk to me about dolares, you will never get to Madrid, never. Your only chance is to go back to France with her."

The two monks spoke to each other. Then the abbot told Michael, "Come with me." He took him to the refectory. "Wait here." On one of the long wooden tables a plate with bread had been left, and Michael hastily put some pieces in his pocket, and swallowed one.

The abbot came back with a basket. "We have little in Spain. Our war is just over and now there is more war all around us. This jug has wine. These are aspirinas. Iodine we have not, but this little bottle has alcohol. A bandage. The bowl has cold rice. A glass. A spoon. The boy will bring a lamp later."

"Thank you. Thank you. But—"

The abbot waved his hand to interrupt him. "Please. This is our charity. Tomorrow you must take the woman with you. It cannot be otherwise."

Michael thought, it would be her death, I have to win him over. He said, "She can't walk. It is as simple as that. You'd better warn the Guardia Civil then to come and arrest us."

The abbot shook his head. "You still do not understand. If the Guardia is called now, they will ask us why we waited so long. This basket here is enough to put me in prison. They may arrest us all. And they will shoot you and the woman, or more likely, hand you over to the Germans. I do not want the monastery to be connected in this. Your only chance is to go back to France. I am giving the woman one more day to rest."

Michael took the basket without another word or look at the abbot, and hurried back to the shed. Marie was lying with her eyes open, a flicker of a smile, or perhaps a grimace of pain, passed over her face. He lifted her head and made her drink some wine and water and swallow several aspirins. He washed the wound with watered down alcohol and bandaged it as well as he could. She fell asleep again.

He sat on the earthen floor and looked at the girl. Again he asked himself, how the hell did I get into this. I'm a soldier right now, that's bad enough, bad enough as an undertaking, getting killed is fifty-fifty for commandos, they say. That is enough for a man. I didn't sign up to be a Saint Bernard dog or Florence Nightingale.

Darkness fell over the sparse landscape. Soon he could only distinguish the outline of the window, a black square with just a hint of grayness. He listened to her breathing. Every time it became irregular, he cringed. A knock on the door of the shed. He found a boy standing there with a burning oil lamp he handed over to Michael.

He took off his shoes finally and got straw to wrap around his feet. He put his raincoat back on. He ate some rice and tried to keep his mind a blank.

When Marie called him, it was night, he had fallen asleep. "I have to pee," she muttered. He carried her to the corner where the floor was covered with straw and held her up, she kept her eyes closed and didn't speak another word. She leaked on his raincoat. When she was finished, he put her back on the cot and covered her. Her bandage hadn't shifted. Then he lay down on the ground and blew out the lamp.

Michael, in 1941

24

The new day started with a clear sky but soon clouds started rolling in again from the mountains to the northwest. Michael had wrapped Marie in her blanket and she was sitting up. "I'll be all right, Michael," she announced several times. They drank water and wine and he made her eat some spoonfuls of rice.

"It is five kilometers to Figueras," he told her. "We will take it very slowly. They have a doctor there, and a pharmacy too, I'm sure." He didn't say anything about the doctor being an army officer. I'll play the American card for all it's worth, he thought. I'll talk to him about our powerful consul and payment in mucho dollars.

"Okay, Mary, here we go." He had made her a walking stick from a broken broom and supported her with his right arm around her middle. They came out of the shed; there was no one in sight. Slowly they followed the path to the gate. The bastards are hiding, he thought. Perhaps they're ashamed.

As Michael tried to open the gate with his left hand, he lost his hold on her for a moment. She uttered a soft moan like a cat, and sank to the ground.

"Goddammit!" Michael screamed, he lifted her up in his arms and turned to the front door of the monastery. He kicked the door as hard as he could, staggering on his feet. A monk opened and jumped aside as he stomped into the hallway with Marie in his arms. "You bastards," he shouted, "you pious hypocrites, phony Christian fascists. This girl needs a doctor, now."

The monk who had opened the door stared at him and took off. Michael was left standing in the hallway, spewing a stream of curses, holding the girl. Marie whispered through his shouts, "Please, please, Michael—you just scare them—let's—"

"Let's *what*?"

"Borrow a cart. Une bruette—what do you call it—a wheel, a wheel—" She started to cry, great wild sobs.

The white-robed abbot had appeared and walked toward them. "I warned you," he said. "I warned you."

If Michael had not been holding the girl in both arms, he would have hit the man. He turned his back to him. One day I'll come back here and shoot the bastard.

Then he heard Marie, speaking in an urgent whisper. "Michael, Michael!"

"What? What?"

"Michael, Michael," she repeated.

That moment he felt so hopeless and worn out that he laid her down on the floor. He kneeled beside her.

She looked up at him and whispered, "Your name is on the wall here. It frightens me so." A confused image raced through her mind, a pogrom, an auto-da-fé, people in robes with flames depicted on them tied to the stake, tablets above their heads listing their names and heresies.

Michael, perplexed, just shook his head, but it was the abbot who came closer to the wall and stared at a tablet affixed there. Then he turned and looked down at Michael who was still kneeling on the floor. He had lost his self-assurance, his hands were trembling. "What is your name?" he asked Michael.

"What the fuck," Michael hissed at him.

The abbot started to say something in Spanish, swallowed, and said, "It is Michel—Michel Beauchamp?"

"Fuck off," Michael said. But Marie held out an arm. "Pull me up, Michael," she whispered. And when she was sitting up she said in an unnaturally loud voice, "Yes! Yes!"

The abbot crossed himself, opened another door in the hall, and said in the same halting voice, "Bring her in here." Then he hurried away.

The room which Michael carried her into was out of place in that Spartan building, it had not only a real bed but also an easy chair, curtains, and paintings on the walls. He put her down on the bed and pulled the bedspread over her. Through all this she had still held on to the broken broom handle.

He closed the door, sat down in the chair, and muttered all the while, "What the fuck, what the fuck."

He felt in the pocket of his raincoat and brought out the pieces of bread he had put in there the day before. He gave her one and she started chewing on it but it was stone-hard. Unexpectedly it made her smile at him, and then she closed her eyes. Not a sound reached them. The wind had risen and through the window he saw the trees swaying. Me and Mary stumbling around out there right now.

Time passed, an hour perhaps, and then the church bells started to ring, on and on. After they had stopped, the abbot entered the room, followed by several monks who stared at Michael and looked self-consciously away from Marie.

"Please to accompany us for a moment," the abbot asked and he and his followers left the room again and waited in the hall. Michael came out to them.

"See this tablet here," the abbot said. "I will translate the Latin into English."

"Thank you, I read Latin." Michael started reading aloud, angrily, "Deo Gratias, Anno—" He read on silently. The monks stood watching him, immobile.

"You know this Michel Beauchamp," the abbot said.

"My grandfather."

A long silence.

"You heard the bells just now, Mr. Beauchamp. We have met in concilium and celebrated a service of thanksgiving."

"Oh. I don't know what you're about."

"We now see the divine interference in your arrival here. We were put to the test and we failed. Yearly we read a mass for this Michel Beauchamp and pray for him but we failed him in you. Now, through the intervention of the wounded woman, a voice spoke to us and saved us from disgracing our order. We gave thanks."

Michael shook his head.

"A miracle," the abbot said. "The wounded woman warned us and yet she was unconscious while she spoke."

Michael did not answer, he read the tablet again. My grandfather, he thought. "Through the sacrifice of—a layman printer from Paris—" Then he was not executed in Paris after all. He escaped. Like us. But this abbot in his shiny whites, I wonder who does his laundry every day, is he now suddenly letting us stay against all those rules of his, is that what he is saying?

"You are changing your sacred rules now and are giving us shelter?" he asked.

"No rules are changed. Divine interference makes your stay

here *extra ordinam,* outside law and dogma. The tablet calls your grandfather a laicus, a Catholic layman, a member of our Mother Church. It is still also your church then."

"I am impressed," Michael answered him, "how you were ready an hour ago to hand a young girl over to the Gestapo and the same treatment for me, and with what ease you've now turned the whole drama into a nice homily."

The abbot looked at the other monks and was obviously assured by their blank faces that they hadn't understood a word. He actually got red in the face, Michael saw. What the hell. I better cool it, this won't help Mary.

"Whatever the reasons, we are assuredly grateful," he ended very formally. "You must now excuse me, I want to get back to the girl. She has a high fever."

"We will speak later."

Michael, in 1941

25

Michael went back to the ornate room where he found Marie asleep. He felt her forehead, was it a bit cooler? He turned the chair and sat looking out. Suddenly one sunbeam shone through a gap in the clouds and made all the glass and crystal in the room glitter. Its air showed itself saturated with dust specks dancing in the sun. Then the light was intercepted again and the sky a menacing, even, black.

His anger and bewilderment were ebbing. By the skin of our teeth, he thought. We have to do some thanksgiving, too. I don't see how the abbot can now refuse to get a doctor, somehow, somewhere, to take the bullet out. She and I are in a real room together, instead of staggering around under that sky. Imagine telling her we have to try and slip back into France. It would have been the end.

No miracle. Surely an astonishing coincidence, saved by my grandfather seventy years later. What was he doing here, why did Anne think he was dead, she never remarried, why didn't he try to find her? When this is all over, if I'm around, touch wood, I must go to Paris, look into archives, solve this riddle.

Or not. It is too late, isn't it, too late forevermore.

He went out into the hallway, leaving the door ajar to hear

Mary, and read the text on the tablet one more time. Michel. Had he really still been a Catholic? A socialist? A dangerous radical, ironically saving one of those parasitical orders from the revolutionaries? He sat down on the floor, leaning his back against the wall. He pressed his eyes shut, trying to see an image of that strange event. "Grand-pére Michel," he whispered.

"I am happy to see you in prayer." The voice of the abbot who stood near him.

"I was trying to understand this man, my grandfather, a Communard, putting himself on the line for this place that—"

The abbot hadn't given up his habit of interruption. "Even if he had been misled by that Commune, as you think, at a crucial moment in his life and in the life of this monastery of the martyr of Lucia, he followed his true heart. Which makes our debt the more. He was wounded by a bullet just like this young woman. He was nursed back to health and shortly after he vanished. But we will measure up to him and do the same for her."

Michael stood up, he put one hand on the tablet (as in an allegorical painting, he thought), seeking to phrase his answer. No more speeches while Mary has a bullet in her body—

But the abbot spoke first. "I have sent for the doctor in Figueras," he said. "That doctor is an officer of the generalissimo's army but he is first a pious man. I have written to him about what happens here and how this is not a matter for the state but for the Church only, a matter *extra ordinam.* He will remove the bullet tonight and he will accept my charging him with silence."

Michael nodded. It seems almost indecent, he said to himself, becoming a player in this medieval fantasy. "I am grateful for your change of heart, sir, for myself and above all for Mary. But I must put myself on record—"

The abbot's hand had gone up again. "I am not surprised at your resistance to open your soul to this. You will no doubt tell yourself that it is all *coincidence.*"

"Yes. I do."

"You're a Latinist," the abbot said, "I have no need to tell you that the Latin *incidere* hides in that English word 'coincidence,' that is, to stumble upon. Do you insist on living in a world where destinies are decided by *stumbling* upon them?"

Not a coincidence then, Michael thought, but that does not make it a miracle, my grandfather and I were both dragged out of our private lives by that Furor Teutonicus which has not changed all that much in those seventy years, nor has Europe in its layout, its human geography. He and I were both on the run to get out of France, away from the Prussians, and into neutral Spain, and there aren't all that many roads squeezed between the Pyrenees and the Mediterranean—

But then he saw himself as he had been wandering around with Mary in the dark hills and how in the end the Santa Lucia was presumably the only place where they could have ended up and not be handed over to the Germans, and asked himself, why couldn't my grandfather's spirit, will, emotions, have steered us here? Nothing preternatural about that, nothing divine, either.

I cannot go with the abbot's "God's will." It is arrogant, and maybe cowardly. A last effort to put humanity back in the center of the universe, where we were kicked out of so long ago by Copernicus and that Dane whose name I forget. But it's okay with me if we willed all this ourselves, if grand-père did. It remains our mystery.

Michael, in 1941

26

Marie and Michael were driven to Figueras in a horse cart by a worker of the monastery. (The monastery truck had been requisitioned early on in the Spanish civil war and never been seen again. All they had left at this time were two cart horses).

Figueras had one train a day to Barcelona. From there they were to travel to Madrid, and on to the narrow-gauge train to Algeciras, final stop on the Southern Railroad, facing Gibraltar across Algeciras bay. The abbot had given them travel vouchers such as the Spanish government handed out in those days to approved institutions, and a hundred pesetas. He had given them a letter with the seal of the monastery that they were traveling on ecclesiastical business.

To crown it all, Michael was now dressed in an old monk's habit, and Marie in the dress of a nun from the French order of Les Soeurs de Cluny which for long forgotten reasons had been hanging in the storeroom.

To such lengths had the abbot now proceeded under that *extra ordinam* flag.

They had been sheltered for eight days until Marie's fever had gone, never talking to anyone but the abbot. The army doctor had come the first evening, he gave Marie morphine and then took the bullet out. Michael had wanted to speak with him but he left unseen by anyone but the abbot. The abbot had also made a point of explaining that Marie's room was not part of the convent but had once been set up for an agronomist in the nineteenth century, in days when the monks used to assist the peasants with their crops.

It was then only two years since Franco had won that civil war he had begun in 1936, and he was still hunting down defeated opponents who were shot or even garroted. Since the 1940 fall of France, the Spanish government had indeed (contrary to what Michael had assumed) handed back dozens of refugees to the Germans. Now it had just begun to receive some essential supplies which the British navy allowed through their blockade, while the Germans provided virtually nothing, as Franco against their expectations stuck to his non-belligerency. At awkward Madrid receptions Spaniards were shaking hands with their British diplomatic colleagues, but out in the real world, *on the ground* as they say, badly paid Spanish policemen and army sergeants still made the rules, escaped English soldiers and pilots were sent back to France, and as for Jewish refugees, they were arrested and expelled as they had been since the year 1492.

There was no gasoline in the country but for the few jerry cans full to drive the generalissimo to his office every day and to enable some favorite general of his to make a motorized entry onto a parade ground. The trains stoked wood and coal in their engines. On the city streets peasant women came to beg, or to sell their homemade bread by the slice on the black market, just as cigarets were sold one at the time. The only booming trade under this regime was prostitution. Soldiers waited in long line for their turn outside the doors of the brothels. They didn't appear to be put off by the traditional apothecary right next door with its big sign in the window saying, simply, SIFILIS. Heaven knows what medication was for sale there; penicillin it was not, that is for sure.

In the year 1941 Spain was still going once more through an only slightly mitigated Middle Ages. That was the country through which Michael and Marie had to make their way to the British outpost at its southern point.

WHEN THE MONASTERY cart reached the streets of Figueras, the driver brought it to a halt and then kept fixedly looking in front of him while Michael and Marie climbed out. The moment Michael had put Marie down on the ground, the driver crossed himself and was off, clearly not happy with the task he had been given and not the least convinced by the abbot's ruling on Church Law. "He looks as if he's making straight for the Guardia Civil," Michael said. Marie didn't listen, she was trying out her leg. Just as well, as she wasn't ready for Michael's jokes. He picked up their bundle and supported her as she hobbled along to the station. "We're doing fine," they told each other.

And they were doing fine, better than they could have dreamt a week earlier. Yet they weren't happy or even cheerful. It had certainly not turned out the lighthearted adventure Michael had promised them on the café terrace in Montpellier. It would have been better if they had hashed it all out, compared feelings, but they did not. Perhaps they were shy to. Marie had lived through her dark moment when it was as if there were no place for her on earth. Michael now felt vulnerable rather than lucky about that sudden rescue.

Paradoxically, the tie between them wasn't strengthened by all this but frayed. There was a silence between them, a kind of hostility almost.

Michael, in 1941

27

The railroad station of Figueras had been left in ruins by the civil war. Planks covered the bomb craters around it and only a corner of the roof had survived. The solitary train to Madrid was due at eight in the evening, and they waited sitting on a low wall in the twilight. No other passengers appeared. The train pulled in almost on time, freight cars and two passenger cars packed with peasants and their boxes and sacks and chickens. A peasant gave up his seat to Marie-as-nun. There was a whistle, agonizingly slowly the train got into motion again, and Michael felt an enormous relief. Finally, finally, they were getting away from that fateful frontier.

They entered Barcelona's Francia station at first light, filthy with soot from the wood-burning train engine and both desperate to find a toilet. But the Guardia Civil patrolling the station didn't even look at them and the buffet sold chicory or maybe it was a corn coffee which was comfortably warm in the misty morning. In their bundle they still had some bread from the monastery.

Marie installed herself in the waiting room with her leg on another chair which did look odd for a nun. "We have to stay awake," she whispered to Michael.

"Yes, we must. I don't think we should go out of the station even. This was a red city, much fighting and killing. I hope you feel strong enough to go straight on to Madrid. I'll go look at the schedule." An express was leaving at ten but he was told their vouchers weren't valid for that; they could leave on the stop-train at noon. He went to tell Marie and then he ventured out onto the station square in hopes of finding some food.

There was a row of vendors on the square and lines for each of them. He waited in one for some kind of reddish soda drink until he realized one had to bring one's own cup or container. At another cart he got four oranges at an outrageous price, and at a sweets cart he found a cake. But when he came back he found Marie shaky and pale.

"Two women came to talk to me," she told him," and when I just shrugged and smiled, they shouted something and then I saw them go and talk to a Guardia Civil. And then he went into some kind of office, just now."

"Oh fuck these fucking bastards. Quick, let's beat it." He helped her up. "There, 'Damas,' a ladies' toilet, stay in there as long as you can. There's bound to be a chair. I'll be sitting on this bench here, watching, and reading my breviary. We'll be okay, you'll see. Try to stay at least till half past eleven!" He had found a breviary in a drawer in Marie's room, and taken it along to help him in his role as a monk.

No one bothered him and when Marie came out it was precisely half past. "I just guessed," she said.

"Let's go to the Madrid platform."

They waited at its far end, amidst bales and crates. Then Michael realized he had left his food purchases on his bench.

Somehow this completely unnerved him. He was banging

his hand on a crate, cursing himself and Franco and the world. "Ssh," Marie kept saying.

"I can't do anything right any more. But I'm not going back. That would just be the thing to screw us up, those fucking women lying in wait there with a cop."

"Michael, please. You make me feel it's me ruining your sang-froid if you know what that is. I don't want you to go back there. I don't need *anything*."

"Sorry," he muttered.

But the noon stop-train turned out to be better than the Barcelona one. They were exhausted enough to sleep, even with all the stops and people cramming in every corner. At one endless stop in the middle of the night Michael got off and came back with a little bottle of wine, and that helped. But Marie's fever had come back.

It was ten the following morning when they got to Madrid, a twenty-two hour journey. The station was like all the others, jostling crowds, crying children, workmen with wheelbarrows and planks pushing through, repairing the bomb damage. "Europe has become so incredibly shabby," Michael whispered to her, "I've been through the blitz but London never looked like this. All those tired and defeated faces." Still, he thought, here I am in the capital of this newly fascist state, really an enemy, it would be quite a thing, being a secret agent here—

"Imagine—" he began, but then he became aware of Marie's face. She looked green, literally, in the sunlight coming in through the cracked glass roof.

"Are you sure you can go on again?" he asked.

"No," she said. "I can't." She spoke very quietly, expecting the worst, possibly no longer caring.

But that made him rise to the occasion. "Poor kid," he said softly, "You've been very tough, not to worry, I'll get you a bed."

"Where?" she muttered.

"There must be a hostel for women near the station, there always are in Europe. Come along, just a few more steps, here we go. Now you're a French nun, on your way to a sister convent in Algeciras. No sweat."

And indeed, at the office of "Ayuda para Damas," Help for Women, in the hall, they sent them to a shelter right across from the station. A cheerful woman who spoke French gave Marie a room for two pesetas, including meals. Michael wanted to help her up the stairs, but the woman said, "I'll do it." And Marie said, "I'll be all right, really." She seemed in a hurry for him to leave. "I'll see you tomorrow then," Michael said.

"Yes." She had been speaking French to him.

So here he was suddenly on his own in Madrid, eleven in the morning, with thirty pesetas in his pocket, as they had divided up the money. He wished he wasn't wearing the monk's robe, he would have liked to sit in a bar or on a café terrace and drink rum or whatever was available and enter, if only in a way, the unknown life of this city; but he didn't dare, you didn't see monks in those places. Anyway, it was a relief to be alone.

He came to a little park, sat down on a bench, and opened his breviary, mumbled some lines, non te extollas in cogitatione animae tuae, I am fucking dying of hunger. He got up and started walking down a little street which had various shops. But their windows were empty and most of the doors locked, except for some places which, as far as he could make out, were offering cleaning or repairs. A grocery had only oranges to offer without ration coupons and they wanted a peseta for one miserable green little thing. A bakery had some nice bread but when he indicated that he had no coupons, they shook their heads and then sold him a horribly sweet pastry for three pesetas fifty. At a barber shop he had more luck, he got a shave for fifty centimos and a haircut for another fifty centimos. He had to fight off the man's efforts to make it very short and give him a tonsure.

"No tonsura?" "No, no. Different order." The barber shrugged, not understanding, but then he even brushed off his robe for him afterward. A shave and a haircut, two bits. He looked at himself in the mirror and decided he was presentable now if you didn't look too closely; he went back to the railroad station and made for the first class waiting room.

It was dark and stuffy in there with the glassless windows boarded up and two gas lamps producing a flickering light that was accompanied by a high buzz. There was a bar with a potted palm on the counter which touched him with its leathery, spooky, leaves, and a barman in a smock covered with mysterious stains who poured him a glass of red wine.

"Por favor. Una tortilla?" Michael asked.

The man silently pointed to a row of little tables. Michael took his glass over to the farthest one, where it was quite dark, and to his surprise the barman brought him a hot omelet there, the best thing, he felt, he'd ever eaten in his life. The bill was fifteen pesetas but he didn't flinch and gave the man a five-peseta tip. Then he curled up on a sofa standing against the back wall and no one bothered him there. He dozed, and watched people saying tearful goodbyes, arguing, lonely men tossing down drinks. When daylight started to show through the cracks between the planks covering the window, he went back to the bar where he got a cup of real coffee for his last pesetas.

Marie looked better, and she said they should go on. "Are you sure you'll be okay?" he asked. I mustn't sound so impatient.

She nodded. She said, quite curtly, "We should get out of this city. Another day is that much more risk, right?"

So they bought two third-class tickets to Algeciras, by way of Granada. It left them with ten pesetas. The clerk pushed the tickets at them under the glass and then said something they did not understand. He acted out a stamping of the tickets and pointed at a sign on a window across from them "Control Fronteriza."

Michael went to look and saw two men in uniform sitting at an empty table, one was rolling a cigarette, the other was yawning and scratching his head. "Let's not go there," he said. "Safer dealing with a train conductor than with two bored cops. Let's go to the platform. Just slow and easy."

But Marie walked better, just slightly leaning on his shoulder. A newspaper boy stood in their path, holding up a copy of a paper; Michael saw a fat headline on the front page, RUSSIA YA VENCIDA, which clearly meant, Russia already beaten. Holy hell. He glanced at Marie but she hadn't noticed, she was walking with her eyes almost closed. When they came to a bench, she asked, "Let's rest for a moment," and he went back to the news boy. A man had just bought a paper and he saw him ignore the front page and turn to a headline on the backpage about futbol. Was he mistaken? He asked the boy, "Russia kaput?"

"Si, si, señor."

The train for Granada, where they'd have to change for the

narrow-gauge, was already at its platform but all doors were locked. A railway man was sitting on an empty luggage cart, and Michael steered Marie toward him and made her show her bandaged leg. "Soror Maria vencida," he told him. The man looked puzzled but then he got up and unlocked the nearest door. The luxury of a whole car of empty seats to choose from. "See, Mary. This must restore your faith in me. We're on the home stretch."

The train never got packed. It rolled through a bare, sun-baked landscape for hours and hours of a summer's day that seemed to have no end. They sank into a stupor, Marie kept shifting her leg, grimacing with pain. She looked haggard again and the fever flush had come back on her pale face.

They got to Granada two hours behind schedule. The little train to Algeciras was pointed out to them and Michael had to half-carry Marie across two platforms, down and up iron staircases. But the spectacle of a shabby monk carrying a lame nun was enough to evoke some sympathy even among their weary fellow passengers. Room was made for Marie in a corner and for him to sit next to her, and an old lady in a nineteen-hundred hat came up to their train window and handed them a bottle of mineral water and a flask of wine. "Gracias, gracias," Michael repeated, squirming under all those smiles suddenly addressed at them. Marie drank the water and most of the wine and it appeared to help her.

IT WAS NIGHT once more, with a half-moon in a black sky when they stumbled out of the Algeciras-Puerto railroad station. No one had asked to see their ticket, let alone any control stamps. No one stirred in the station but the station bar was open and Michael succeeded in buying a tiny bottle of rum, which cleaned them out. He sat with Marie on a broken wooden bench outside the station entrance and they had two sips each. "Lovely," she muttered. "I'm becoming a refuse alcohol—a refugee alcoholic—" She even giggled.

"We must plan our next move," Michael said, but she had fallen asleep with her head against his shoulder. He put an arm behind her and shifted to make her more comfortable. I could steal a rowboat. If that doesn't work, find a fisherman, promise him a reward at the other end. But I can't drag Mary around any more. I could have swum across the bay like Byron—

At the far end of the avenue he could see the glitter of the moonlight on the water of the bay. The air was warm and he could smell the sea. After a while he could make out the soft swish-swish of the waves hitting the quay. They had reached the very tip of Europe.

Michael, in 1941

28

MICHAEL CAME OUT OF HIS HALF DREAM OF OCEAN waves, starlight, sitting on a beach with his date, from far off the sound of his Philadelphia high school band playing, "Blue Moon, you saw me standing alone without a dream in my heart without a love of my own—" A man had loomed up in front of him, intercepting the light of the street lamp. He could just see that he was in uniform. Every man in Europe is in uniform this year, Michael thought. Or in prison stripes.

"Documentación, por favor," the man said in a not unfriendly voice.

Michael pulled his arm back without waking up Marie. He fished out the letter from the monastery. The guardia turned to the rather miserable bit of light from the lamppost and spent a long time studying it. He returned it to Michael. He asked, "Francés?"

"Si."

"Pasaporte?"

Michael shook his head, waved the letter, pointed at its seal.

The guardia held out his arms with the hands turned up, a guesture of apology, it would seem. He signaled Michael that they had to come with him.

At the guardia post they were shown to a waiting room.

Marie, who hadn't spoken a word, stretched out on the wooden floor and was immediately asleep again. Michael sat on a chair and stared out the barred window at a narrow courtyard with a dead palmtree in the middle. Dawn was coming, there was just a glimmer of color in the sky over the roof across from him.

When an officer showed up, it turned out he didn't speak French but English. Michael now decided on his story. He explained to the man that he had been sent to accompany this nun to the military hospital in Gibraltar. She had an infected leg wound and the military doctor in Figueras had told them that the English military doctor in Gibraltar had a new drug that could save her leg.

The officer listened to all this with a blank face. He looked at Marie, still asleep, and even bent over to feel her forehead. "Yes, much fever," he said.

"It would be barbaric to keep her here," Michael told him.

The officer left and after a while two men appeared with a stretcher and carried Marie out. Michael tried to follow but the guardia stopped him. "Momentito," he said.

"Where are they taking her?"

"Hospital. Okay. Wait here."

Presently the same officer reappeared and beckoned Michael to follow him. They went to an office where an elderly man, a civilian, was waiting. "I am interpreter," he told Michael.

The officer talked to the interpreter at some length and then waited for him to translate. "The officer says, we are not barbarians, the French nun is taken to the Gibraltar military hospital. With the police boat. No difficulty. You must wait. The officer wants to know, how are you? Correction. Who are you?"

"I am a scholar from the monastery of Santa Lucia near Figueras. I am from America. I am learning to speak Spanish. I am the escort for Sister Maria and I should have gone with her."

The interpreter related this to the officer and they had a discussion. Michael recognized some words but he couldn't guess if the officer was friend or foe. He tried to look self-assured.

"The officer is not satisfied," the interpreter said. "He must consult his superiors. For now, you will stay here." Michael did not answer.

They put him in a cell in the police station. They gave him a blanket and a towel. Later in the day his door opened and he jumped up, they must have called Madrid, I made it. No, it was just another guardia civil who gave him a bowl of soup and a tin spoon.

BUT DAYS WENT BY, one week, two weeks. Every time the guardia brought him his food (acorn coffee and a chunk of bread at dawn, a bowl of soup midday and at night), he asked the man, "El interprete?" and the man always smiled and shrugged and never spoke a word. And Michael would ask, "Books? Libra? Paper?" acting out reading and writing, also without result.

Perhaps these men weren't cruel, perhaps they simply didn't relate to his being there. Since five years now their prisoners had been less than fellow human beings, they had been people first to be beaten up and tortured if some information was to be gotten out of them, and then to be killed. This alien young man who seemed to be a monk but possibly wasn't, who seemed neither on their side nor on the enemy's side, was outside their ken.

After some weeks they started to leave his cell door unlocked some of the time and thus he could walk up and down the corridor between two gates and go to the john without a guard (it was a pilgrim's toilet, but still a lot better than the filthy bucket in his cell).

Nothing from the outside world was visible but a few square feet of sky through a high window. There was nothing to read for him but a French poem an earlier prisoner had scratched on the wall and that began, "Vous n'aurez ni l'Alsace ni la Lorraine, car malgré vous nous resterons français—" He wondered if he should try going on a hunger strike, but after five years of war they probably wouldn't give a damn and just let him die quietly. And he had been so close, goddammit, he had been within reach of the bay, he could have swum across. He endlessly repeated, "Vous n'aurez ni l'Alsace—" It was not to be believed, stuck at the edge of a million square miles of torture and death dealing, in a plague of hatred and willed misery set off by a psychopathic German noncom. Seen from England it was easier, the Germans simply had to be killed, but here in Europe on their home ground it was all interwoven, they would tear down the whole shebang with them. Did the Germans actually want to win, and live lives as in some ghastly science fiction story, a slave empire run with modern machines, with German managers over hordes of illiterate, castrated, underfed serfs? How much unhappiness the Germans have caused us in this century!

Summer ended, the nights became bitter cold. Time now lost its reasonability. He was descending into an opaque world. He was also unbelievably filthy and had grown a beard soft to the touch, the hairs were that long.

At times, in the night, he thought that he should be satisfied if this imprisonment never ended. If being alive is a blessing within itself, he had been blessed by having been taken out of time. A year will be a century. I'll be as near as one can get to immortality.

In the early mornings, when he sat on his bunk with his eyes fixed on the high window opening, waiting for the first color to enter the black square of the sky, when he felt some strength in his arms and legs, he said to himself, or sometimes shouted, "It's impossible! Intolerable!" and he'd bang on his cell door and shout, "Help! Help!" There was never a response, not even an echo.

Regrets. He listed all his regrets and if's, beginning and ending with his not swimming across the bay to Gibraltar. Drowning would have been so very much preferable over this. But could he have left Mary, sleeping on that bench? But why wasn't she trying to help him now? Why the silence? Why hadn't he gone to the British in Madrid, and thrown himself at their mercy? If he had only charmed that American woman in Vichy instead of swearing at her—

And why had Anne thought that her husband had been shot? Michel—had he not tried to get to America? It would have been the logical safe place for him, the new, rebellious republic as it was then. Or had he been locked away in solitary somewhere, as he was now? Was there a meaning in Michel saving him and he then repeating his fate? Was Mary his Anne? Hardly. Unless her silence was like Anne's silence once.

On and on, until he fell asleep and often dreamt about execution pelotons in which he was both part of the detail with the rifles and one of the poor devils tied to a stake, blindfolded, and waiting in that dark for the bullets to bite through his skin.

A morning came when he was not given his tin cup of imitation coffee. The hours went by. He felt a cold fear now that they had simply forgotten him, that he was the last man in this dank building. I'll slowly starve, he thought. But so what. I'll pretend it's by choice, pretend I opted for that hunger strike.

He stroked his beard and he began to laugh. This idiotic beard. I wonder how I look. I'm the Count of Monte Cristo. Ha ha! If I go on laughing, hysterically, they'll take me to the hospital or to a madhouse, whatever, it will give me a chance to escape. He forced himself to go on laughing, walking up and down with heavy steps. Then he realized a guard was standing in the corridor, staring at him. He couldn't go on, he sat down.

The man came to the cell door now. He still didn't open it. "Lavar, por favor," he said, acting out the washing of his face. Then he handed Michael a parcel with a piece of soap, a rusty Gillette shaver with a blade in it, nail scissors, a used toothbrush, and a new towel.

Later the same man came to inspect him. He nodded his approval. Michael had shaved, a long and painful process, brushed his teeth and washed his face and hands. The rest of his body remained hidden inside his filthy robe.

After the midday soup another guard showed up and took Michael to the office where he had once been questioned by the officer. He motioned him to sit down and posted himself near the door.

Waiting. The sun had come around to the window and Michael shifted his chair to get some warmth from it. He was always freezing now. But his heart was beating in his throat. Something was happening. I swear, he said to himself, I'll be as cold as ice. No matter what they have in store for me.

Voices were heard in the corridor. The door opened and an English voice said, "After you, sir." A Spanish officer came in, a big fish with lots of gold braid. And after him a man in a British naval uniform.

Michael stood up and looked at him, silently.

"Miguel Bocam?" the Spanish officer asked, looking at a document.

Michael nodded.

"You are released into our custody," the British officer said. "You have to sign their papers and then I can take you with me."

Michael closed his eyes. He thought that this darkness and silence was his true reality, not what was happening around him.

"Perhaps you should go and get your kit," he heard the British officer say.

He opened his eyes. "I haven't any."

"Oh. Well, we better be on our way then."

Walking down to the quay under a blue sky. "I'm lieutenant Davis," his companion said.

At the quay a little patrol boat flying the British White Ensign was waiting, a British military policeman and a guardia civil together posted at the gang plank. When the MP saw Davis approaching, he flicked his cigarette into the water. A moment later Michael was standing on the deck. He remained motionless and had nothing to say. Davis offered him a cigarette but he refused because his hands were shaking too much. He thought he'd not ever forget the feel of the sun and the breeze on his face. He wished the crossing would go on for hours, he could not think beyond it.

When they tied up at the Gibraltar mole, he was dizzy and Davis had to steady him. "You're going to see lieutenant-commander Willers," he said. "Follow me."

"What time is it?" Michael asked. Knowing the time of day again seemed a symbol to him, a new dispensation.

"Three o'clock," Davis said. "And by the way, welcome back on British soil."

Michel, after 1873

29

On his first day in Tunis, Michel found himself a job at the Café de Paris. Its owner had calculated that the glamor attached to a Legion veteran and *mutilé de guerre* would outweigh the bother of having a waiter with one arm. It was a fancy, European-style place and the man treated anyone and anything that wasn't French with contempt. Michel told him that he had lost his right arm "in the fighting for Biskra." His wage wasn't much but he was told that he could keep all his tips, and he had rented a room above a bookshop at the edge of the European quarter.

The first week in the Café de Paris was a good time for him, it was so different that it made it easier not to dwell on the past. He had a Parisian's love for café life and it was intriguing to see it from the other side of the fence; he had to work four hours at lunchtime and five hours in the evening, with Sundays off. He started, hesitantly, to believe in the chance of starting a new life one day, not in France surely but in America maybe. I'd turn my back on Europe then, he thought. I must save money here, and teach myself sufficient English. The loss of his arm did not loom very large in his daily thinking.

The first payday, Saturday after closing, took some of the

bloom off. He was now informed that yes, he could keep his tips, but he had to contribute to "the overhead of the service," to be determined by the maitre d' and about a third of all the tips at his station. Never mind, he told himself, I won't stay long. Here he had looked forward to a simple life, for a whole year maybe, saving money, and after one week that was already not what he was at. But he had decided not to feel sorry for himself, and he wasn't.

Once he had learned the café routine, the code words for the most popular dishes and the wines most profitably recommended, the work became a tiring but almost automatic routine. In the beginning he had winced at being addressed as "garçon," boy, but soon enough that became a code word too. The guests were more polite with him than with the other waiters, anyway.

One evening a Frenchman asked him, "Say, garçon, the owner tells me you lost your arm at Biskra. Now I'm an army colonel and I had always thought that Biskra was taken in 1850. Aren't you a bit young to have been there?"

The man had a jeering tone of voice and his manner and face suddenly reminded Michel of Henri Labin, the ivory merchant. He stared at him. And only then did it come to him: Labin must have been the informer. He must have gotten hold of that letter of his from Vichy, he must have gone to the police after he had come face to face with him in Paris. He stood motionless, holding his tray, a buzz in his head.

The voice of the colonel penetrated the fog. "Well, fellow, what of it? Your arm, man, your arm."

"I must get him," he stammered, "I must—I must." But then his head cleared and he fell silent. He stared at the colonel and the colonel stared back at him. "Colonel, let me suggest that you go and fornicate with your grandmother," he said and walked away.

After closing, he was told he was fined a week's wages for insulting a guest, and from then on the owner was as sharp with him as he was with the other personnel.

EVERY SUNDAY Michel walked to the Tunis hospital where an arm prothesis was made for him. The technician involved was an Arab, chosen because he worked on the Christian Sunday which was Michel's only free day. The man did the job with great care and with weekly fittings. It would cost Michel two gold twenty-franc pieces. (The money of Tunisia was a shambles of piasters and dinars, and foreigners and people such as the customers of the Café de Paris were expected to pay in francs or English pounds). Those two gold pieces, *louis d'or* as they were called, were as much as Michel made in a month, after the deduction of the "overhead" plus the two francs for renting his waiter's tuxedo from the café.

On the weekend of the European Easter, the Café de Paris was to be closed for two days. On Good Friday, Michel's prothesis was finally finished and declared a perfect fit by his maker. It would soon stop hurting, he assured Michel. He couldn't move the fingers, of course, but for that period it was very good, with one hinge at the elbow and one at the wrist. The hand was made of wood and Michel had bought thin white gloves to wear. He was pleased and set out to celebrate that he looked a whole man again, as he called it to himself.

This was the first time he came away from the quarter where he worked and slept. He walked to the shore of the little lake that lies between Tunis and the Mediterranean and took the ferry which sailed back and forth across it to Tunis's port,

Goletta. In Goletta he circled the fortress but kept his eyes down, waiting until he had found a bench. Only then did he raise his eyes and looked at the sea.

There, once more, she lay before him, the free sea. Thalassa! After the claustrophobia of his years on the run, of prisons, army barracks, those long gray corridors of the hospital where they had amputated his arm, after those locust years, here was the sea, a sea like the sea he had been born near to in Le Havre.

He was free. He could ship out to any place on earth.

It was then that he decided to save even more stringently, to focus on this one goal: flee the bitterness, the disillusions of the old world.

He took a deep breath and looked around him with a smile. At the other end of his bench a young woman was seated, she was eating a brownish porridge from a bowl and taking sips from a bottle of water. Their eyes met and she smiled.

That smile surprised him very much. Here he was in a threadbare white shirt, a pair of tuxedo trousers they had been about to throw away at the café, and his idiotic white gloves—I must look most unpleasant. And she, very clean black hair, a flowery dress, a fine face—a girl for a spring walk in the woods of Ville d'Avray.

"You are not treating yourself very well," he called out to her. "That looks like prison food, dry couscous and water."

She answered in a mocking tone, "You don't mean to say you have been in prison, sir?"

It took him aback. He moved closer to her. "I have, but not as a thief."

"I know, you're a nihilist." She laughed.

Michel wondered about those words. His idea of abstaining from the modern world, was that akin to nihilism? "Perhaps I am," he answered gravely, "but I didn't see it like that. I have left that political banquet of ideas where we poison ourselves with unhappiness."

"I know. You are a professor."

"I am a waiter at the Café de Paris."

She took another bite of the stuff in her bowl and made a face. "Now you've spoiled it for me."

"But what are you?" he asked.

"Oh me. I'm a Belgian lady of fortune. A schoolteacher, right now."

"In the meantime, a growing girl cannot live on couscous and water. Why don't you come with me to the café. It's closed today but the caretaker will let me in. We can sit in the kitchen and I will serve a lunch of haute cuisine leftovers."

Again she surprised him by immediately agreeing. "An offer I can't refuse," she said.

There was a catch in his voice as on their way back to town he tried to keep up a conversation. He had to force himself not to hold her arm, not to touch the curve of her neck above the white collar of her dress.

In the kitchen of the café he put two chairs at the little table which the chef used to write his memos. He heated up a pan of stew (lapin chasseur) for them. The wine cellar was locked but he found an open bottle of Médoc, still three-quarters full, on the shelf where the chef kept his notebooks. They ate in almost complete silence but he kept smiling at her and she smiled back.

She must have been aware of the tension and haste of his movements but did not comment on it. He walked her to the house where he had his rented room, he unlocked the front door and she went ahead of him up the stairs. They stood in his room. He tugged at the window curtains which didn't quite close and then with trembling fingers tried to unbutton her dress with his left hand. He turned away and took his clothes off, but he kept his shirt on because of his arm. He tried to wait, to caress her, but he couldn't, he fell on top of her. "I apologize," he whispered afterward.

"We'll do it again more slowly," she said, stroking his hair.

"What's your name—"

"Danielle." She didn't show any reaction to his wooden arm.

When she left, she didn't say a word about seeing each other again. It pleased him, he had been worried about it, about how it could intervene with his plan to save, to focus on leaving, and nothing else.

But that same evening, sitting on his windowsill and looking down into the empty street, he thought what a fool he had been for letting her go without even asking where she lived. Here was a woman miraculously attracted to him in his present state, and he hadn't even had the sense to walk her home.

He turned his head toward the room which was already in shadows, and looked at his bed still in disarray. He saw her lying there, naked, and it seemed too unlikely to have been true. I will wait for her next Sunday on that bench at the harbor, he thought. She will reappear. She may like me better for not having been too pressing.

DANIELLE WAS NOT a schoolteacher, she was an inmate of the famous Maison Latouche on the Bal-el-Minar, one of the handsomest streets of Tunis with its triple row of palm trees. It was a *maison close*, the most expensive brothel of the town. Sunday was her day off and she had promised herself to spend it alone. But Michel's naiveté, and that setting, the bench almost surrounded by the sunny sea—it had all added up to make her feel very light and carefree. As long as I don't accept any money, she thought, I didn't really break my promise, it isn't a stint.

Michel, after 1873

30

When the European Easter holiday was over, Michel paid a visit to the little bookshop on the ground floor of his building. It was run by a Frenchwoman who told Michel she had learned English from her father who gave her English newspapers to read. "It was a marvelous system," she told him. "But now I've forgotten everything."

She found a cheap English-French dictionary for him, it was printed in 1826 and had any number of odd words and expressions, but it would serve his purpose, she assured him.

During the afternoon break at the café, he walked over to The Palace, the first hotel of Tunis. It had come down in the world but was still the place where American and British travelers stayed. They had a kiosk with foreign newspapers and he found a yellowing three-months old copy there of the Paris Herald. The concierge promised to keep a copy of a new Herald for him when they came in.

Between seven and eight in the evening, when the air was cooling but before the restaurant customers started to arrive, the young waiters of the Café de Paris used to sit outside the back entrance smoking. Two old waiters considered this beneath their dignity and stayed in. Michel belonged to neither group but he sat on the steps with his Paris Herald and his dictionary, spelling out the articles, not talking to anybody. And one evening later that week, to his great joy, he looked up from his paper to see Danielle go by on the sidewalk across the street from him.

He ran over. She was heavily made up and looked elegant, a different creature from the girl in the flower dress with her bottle of water.

"Danielle—I am happy to see you! I was mortified when I faced the fact that I could not get in touch with you."

"Oh—we would have met again on our bench, I think. That is where I have my Sunday lunch, al fresco."

She did not seem pleased to see him, he thought. Can't blame her, she's off to some elegant party and here I am in shirtsleeves between the garbage cans. She's waiting to get away.

"Well, nice to find you again," he said. "Perhaps you want to make a date—have dinner with me next Sunday? A real one, not in the kitchen here?"

She smiled then. "All right," she said and started walking on.

"Where? Where will we meet?"

She turned her head to him. "On my bench, at eight."

Once or twice a week he went over to the Palace Hotel now for a conversation with the concierge. It had begun when the man refused to be tipped for saving him a Paris Herald. "You are of the profession," he said. "People like us must stick together." He was an odd concierge; long ago he had been a tax assessor in Lyon, he told Michel, "but I made a mistake and had to get away double quick."

Michel now got the idea that The Palace was the place to take Danielle to dinner the following Sunday. "I have to impress a girl," he told his new friend. "She came by in a party dress and there I was sitting in my shirtsleeves on the kitchen steps of the Paris. She was not amused."

"Leave it to me. I'll reserve you a table in the bar, that's less chi-chi. We'll tell 'em to hold the bill and I get you a house price, a prix d'ami."

"It's very nice of you."

"Listen, my friend, it's all part of the game. You'd be surprised how many of our high and mighty guests in their cutaways get reduced rates. 'Get me a carriage for the gala, Albert, we managed to get tickets.' Yeah, two freebies because your brother-in-law has the cigarette concession. I see them in their underpants, Michel. Not literally, thank God, figuratively."

So now all Michel had to do was getting a white bow tie instead of the black one a waiter wears with his evening clothes, and he'd look a man-about-town, at least from a distance, he said to himself. The following Sunday he sat on the Goletta bench at halt past seven all decked out; it had been a long time that he had done a thing like that.

Danielle showed up, in the same flower dress of their first meeting, and acted out stunned surprise, holding her hand over her wide-open mouth. "My, you're pretty," she said with a grin.

"Wait till you hear where we are going for dinner. You know the Palace Hotel?"

"Yes. Don't tell me that's where you want to take me."

"But I do. It's all arranged."

"I'm sorry, but no. You were sweet to think of it, don't be disappointed. I hate those places. It's my day off, I don't want to stare at a lot of fat men stuffing themselves and snapping their fingers at the waiters. What a waste of money."

"Oh."

"Cheer up, I'll take you to a cozy little joint. You'll see."

THEIR SUNDAY DINNER became a fixed date. They took turns paying. Danielle insisted on that; George Sand was her heroine, she told Michel, an independent spirit. She tried to become one herself. Had he heard of George Sand? He smiled. "Yes indeed, I printed—"

"What?"

"No, never mind."

Most Sunday nights Danielle stayed with him but she refused to talk about her job or even tell him where she lived. Then there were the times when she started to say something, stopped herself, and refused to finish the sentence. If Michel insisted, she became angry which was most unusual for her.

All this filled Michel with a vague apprehension: he had become someone who expects the worst. Perhaps she was married with a husband who was away on Sundays, and that meant that one day she would vanish, without warning, without appeal, as Anne had.

Then came a Monday morning when he gave her a goodbye kiss in his room, as he had to go to the café early; he went on his way and suddenly stopped. He walked back to the building where he lived and posted himself in a doorway. When Danielle came out, he followed her.

He knew that if she saw him, she'd never forgive him. What he was doing was destructive, worse: ignoble. But he couldn't resist it.

She entered the villa quarter of Tunis and walked down the Bal-el-Minar. He was astounded, he had never been there and hadn't known Tunis had such royal streets, shaded by towering palm trees. She went up the steps of a mansion, and then she vanished. He waited a long time, finally he walked up to that door himself. He stared at the gleaming brass knocker, touched it, turned around.

As he came down the steps, a horse and cart came to a halt in front of the house, and the driver took a crate off his cart and carried it down the service steps. Michel waited and saw an old Chinese servant open the door and then step aside to let the man carry it in. He looked up and saw Michel standing there, in his tuxedo, staring at him. He said, "The house opens at six only, sir."

"The house?"

"This house. Maison Latouche."

The waiters at the café regularly discussed the brothels of Tunis and the commissions to be earned from sending them customers. Michel had heard everthing about Maison Latouche, the prices, the jokes, the famous customers. His only thought now was, not to be seen by her. He rushed off, to his work. I'll think about this all later. I must be at the café, they're expecting me early. But presently he turned around and went back to his room instead.

Michel was not, as the expression has it, "a man of his times." In a sense he was a man of the best of his times. He believed in *égalité* which was more than is implied in the English word equality, and, rare at that time, for him it included women as a matter of course. He had had his jealousies but he had always seen them as an archaic disease, a remnant of a primitive sense of property. Now, different from most of his contemporaries, he didn't think that Danielle being a whore made her immoral and corrupt; the idea didn't enter his mind. She was one of the myriad victims of the corrupt and immoral nineteenth century, supposedly humanity's crowning achievement.

And the idea that more likely than not she would one day end up penniless in the Salpetière Hospital of Paris was unbearable. He thought that now he felt love for her but did not want to make love to her, he wanted to *avenge* her. He would have wanted to be able to rush over to that damn villa with its damn palm trees and take her in his arms and console her, he would want to buy her a house in Ville d'Avray and swear that no man, including himself, would ever again lay an unwanted hand on her. It was all rather exalted and Danielle might have shrugged it off if she had heard it, but a man who had been locked up in his body for so long now, was vulnerable to exaltation.

And he cursed himself for his vanity, his idiotic pride, thinking that this young woman somehow had found him attractive, in his shabby clothes and his wooden arm, because she had immediately accepted his invitation. That was the most painful, perhaps.

He fled his little room and went to the shore of the lake. He lay down on the burned grass and stared up at the harsh blue sky.

When he showed up at the Café de Paris the following morning, he was told he was fired. But the same day he found another job, in a dingy place on the edge of the Arab town. It was called Las Tapas but the owner, a Spaniard, had long stopped serving tapas which are Spanish hors d'oeuvres. At his bar sat serious drinkers from early in the day on, and the badly lit restaurant was popular with dubious middle-aged men who came to have bad meals there with their unshaven business partners and with young girls they said were their daughters. This time Michel got no wage at all but he could really keep the tips which varied from nothing to a gold louis d'or from a happy drunk. He had to work every day of the week, but when he had told the Spaniard that he had to go see his mother Sundays at midday, the man had only shrugged which could very well have meant, all right by me.

On his first Sunday he had gone to the port early and took time reading the names of the ships and their home ports on the sterns. At that time Goletta could only handle small ships and there wasn't one from farther away than Marseilles, but several were from Naples which was just across the water, and a port for ships to everywhere.

Around noon he went to sit at one of the outdoor tables of an Arab café where he was silently brought a cup of coffee and then ignored. The hour he had there was the best of that miserable week. He saw himself as from very high up: a shabby man sitting on a kitchen chair on the sidewalk of a narrow street at the end of the world, his little empty cup with the dried-up traces of its previous users, in a total anonymity to the men and women passing by. He was truly lost, and there was a certain peace in that.

He slowly walked to land's end as he called it, hesitant, and stopped at the corner of the square where the bench was. She was there, unwrapping something to eat, a bottle of water beside her, just as the first time.

He walked over and sat beside her without saying anything, just holding her hand. He was afraid of speaking, he thought that if he had to, he would burst into tears. Her sitting there, which before had seemed so sunny and carefree, now showed itself as endlessly pathetic, a young woman already defeated by the hasty cruelty of the world.

She didn't seem surprised by his odd behavior, but held his hand tightly. The sea was gray now, with white foam heads. "Even the sea is sad today," she finally said.

"Yes."

"I'm going to France soon, Michel," she said. "I wrote a letter to George Sand and I now have good hope that she will help me. Did you know she is a baroness?"

"I was a book printer once, long ago. I printed some of her first novels. I remember, what was it, 'The Sin of Monsieur Antoine.'"

"Oh—that doesn't sound like her. She doesn't believe in sin."

"It was not about cheating husbands and wives. It was about political sin. She was a real socialist then, a Red."

"But she's a baroness," Danielle said indignantly.

He smiled. "Nonetheless. I assure you."

Then there was another long silence. "What's wrong, Danielle?"

"Nothing."

She must have seen me, he now realized. He recalled those tall decorated windows, the balconies, of the Maison Latouche—hadn't he seen the curtains move? Should I tell her—tell her what?

"Listen, Danielle. Did George Sand really answer your letter?"

"Yes. Well, not directly. But a friend of a friend of hers told me that she rarely does, but that she said she was interested in me and that my letter showed spirit. I am sure it is going to be all right."

"Listen. I've a new job, in another café, big shabby cantina, but all right. Now last night there was a captain at the bar, or anyway a sailor who said he was a captain, he was a smuggler and very far gone. And he gave me a hundred-franc note for a tip. One of his friends tried to take it back from me but he noticed and he shouted to him to leave me alone."

"How nice for you, Michel."

"Well, I brought it. I want to give it to you. It'll pay your train ticket to where Sand lives, that little house in Berri, I can't think of the name right now."

"Nohant."

"Of course. Nohant."

That cheered him up, that she knew the name. Possibly it's all true then and there's a happy ending for her.

"But I don't want your money. I don't need it." she said.

"Please. It isn't my money. It's pirate money. It will bring you good luck."

"Listen," he said, "We can't have our dinner, I have to get back to my Tapas cantina. It's a seven days a week job. Next Sunday—will you still be here?"

"Yes, but some friends will come and help me pack. I'm leaving that week."

"So this is goodbye then," he asked.

"Give me a kiss, Michel."

Michel, in 1873

31

Tunis was a silent town, those last few years of the 1870s, before the French army and navy showed up and turned Tunisia into a colony of France. It was a town of white stone and empty streets under the burning sun (and at rare times under wild rain and hail), white, white, white. Within that blanchness sharp little islands of color stood out, of men in yellow or blue djelabas talking in the shade of stone walls or palm trees, of men slurping from cups of coffee never lifted to their mouths but held still and upright, men under turbans of red and white, green for the very pious. Color, also, of the occasional red, white, and blue door indicating a public bath.

All those men, and the merchants sitting behind their wares in the souks, had long beards and looked to Michel as grave and wise as Old Testament prophets or Greek philosophers wondering about human life, while they might actually be sitting there trying to decide whether to buy another cup of coffee or use the money for a candied egg yoke—how would one know?

A world so far removed from us in time and space, so still, that we could have thought we were watching life after death. And even for Michel who was himself born in a world virtually without machines except for clocks (France in the 1840s), this

Tunis became unfathomable. Once his mourning Anne had become a permanent but muted tone in his sound spectrum, he lost that cocoon which in those days enveloped white people setting forth into an unconquered part of what is now called the Third World.

He thought of Gutierre; seeking shelter in a monastery without the faith that has to go with it seemed an idle enterprise. He still believed in his plan to voyage to Naples one day and from there on, into the world. He still read the Paris Herald with his dictionary. His savings were minimal so far but his Tapas boss hadn't fired him. In fact, his silence, and his eyes which seemed focused inward, earned him a certain respect in that society. He functioned. And he had odd moments of a painful clarity when he saw himself as play-acting and thought that a day would come when he would simply decide to be himself again.

His routine remained unchanged. He worked seven days a week in the restaurant but disappeared at odd hours on Sundays, when he went to sit on the bench in Goletta. He had no friends, he had stopped his chats with the Palace concierge when he realized the man was embarrassed about his shabby appearance. Danielle remained the last woman who had shared her body with him. His face was drawn and he looked much older than his age now. He went on walks, one of them to a Lebanese money changer who wrote down the deposits of his savings in a leather-bound book.

And there were nights which found him wandering the dead streets of the southern quarter of the town, the Bab-el-Djazera, when he was afraid to go to his sleepless little room. Walking there when the rays of the late moon reflected in the house walls made him think he was walking in the light of purgatory. He felt then as if his own mind was leaching out of him, his blood turning white.

A sense of panic that he would not ever leave Tunis. He had to get more money and why shouldn't he go about it by making himself known? He thought again about that Greek exile quoting the Odyssey in the market, and about Ovid, the poet, an exile like he himself. He sat up one night with a notebook and managed to write down many lines of the "Tristia" from his memory. Those are the verses Ovid wrote when he was banned from Rome to a muddy village on the Black Sea.

It started out as a game but presently it became real. He was not a tramp and he was not really a Legion veteran; he was an exile, one of a band of brothers, men punished for their words and their thoughts. He too, like that Greek exile, should make himself known, make them understand why he was there, while they could call him "garçon" and toss him a franc. This ground he would stand on here was as ancient as Greece, it was Carthage. Someone, a European archeologist perhaps, or an Arab scholar, would recognize him, ask him to his home, have him bathed and fed. They would have long discussions, and then a time would come when his new friend would say, "You must let me send you to America. You may repay me one day if you want to."

That Sunday he sat himself on a little wall outside the St. Louis Chapel. It was the only Christian church in Tunis, but he had chosen it especially because it was on a height called "the French hill." He did not feel embarrassed; to the contrary, this would finally fit his station. He stared in the distance, and he began quoting the poet, "Cum subit illius tristissima noctis imago."

Several passers-by tossed him a caroube, a small local coin, and some children stopped to stare at him from a safe distance.

The church bells started to ring, and he waited.

He continued saying those words in his mind, "The most sad image of that night," the last night of Ovid's life in his city, Rome, and he fell into a reverie, how much that night must have seemed the "Now" to him and how tracelessly it had vanished. How short is the life of a human being in time. And how modern, or perhaps better, how timeless it sounded, that "his last night in Rome." Like a travel story in a Paris newspaper. But it was two thousand years ago, and he felt an overwhelming pity for that man, and a hatred, no, contempt, for the powers on this earth who dare do these things to their fellow men and women.

The church bells stopped and he stood up on top of the wall. He raised his voice as loud as he could, and began speaking the verses—"as my last hours in the city fled away"—that was Paris, and Anne, he thought.

A boy threw a stone at him but he ignored that. Then the churchgoers were coming out and he forced himself to look them in the face as they approached him. But now no one even tossed him a coin. They looked away, uneasily, and gave the wall a wide berth.

It didn't faze him. The poet is now my brother, he thought.

Michel, after 1873

32

It was winter again. On a cold, sunny, day he was sitting on his Goletta bench. He had brought a stack of Herald newspapers to go through once more.

> BEAUCHAMP. Anne Beauchamp of Philadelphia. Beloved widow of Michel Beauchamp who was a renowned Paris printer. A private funeral has taken place. A Mass will be said in the Church of St. James, Chestnut Street, Philadelphia, on Sunday, May 17, at 11 o'clock in the morning.

He shook his head, he could not comprehend what he had read. "Death Notices," it said at the top of the page. May 17. But that was six months ago. I missed it.

He tore the paper into little pieces and then he began to shake like a man with a palsy. He rushed back to his room. I will stay in here now, he thought, I will not go to to work, I will not go anywhere.

Here I was sitting with my newspapers. Studying English to go to America. And she was there. She was there. She was alive. How did she die so young there? Could I have saved her? Did she lose our child? Now I am too late, too late forever.

One early morning, perhaps the following day, perhaps

much later, he had just fallen asleep after a night of thinking, when he was awakened by cannon fire. For one single, eternally endless, blissful, moment he was in bed with Anne, in his Paris bombarded by the Germans. He laughed aloud from happiness.

Then he was back in Tunis. He jumped up and went out into the street in his torn nightshirt.

"What is happening?" he asked several passers-by but they glared at him and hastened on. An old sailor whom he used to serve absinthes in the café did stop and told him, "The French have landed. There's a French squadron lying off Goletta. They say the Bey is held prisoner in his own palace."

Michel hurried to Goletta, running most of the way, on bare feet, once he lost first one then the other slipper. People quickly stepped aside for him. So they've come for me, he thought. I am glad.

He saw the gray shapes of warships in the distance. A sloop, flying the French flag, was made fast to the pier, two marines with fixed bayonets stood guarding it. He went up to one of them.

"Here I am, the man you have been looking for all this time," he said. "I'm ready."

"Step back, fellow," the marine said.

Michel came closer. "I'm not your fellow," he said slowly. "I am the renowned Paris printer. And you are the men who murdered my Anne."

As he slapped the man's face, the other marine took the regulatory step forward, bent his knee as he had been taught, and stuck his bayonet in Michel's back.

Michel turned and saw that the marine was holding a tablet, "Deo Gratias—our brother Michel—" and then he died.

Michael, in 1941

33

Gibraltar. Michael followed lieutenant Davis through long corridors in the rock. They came to a door with the sign, Lieutenant-Commander H. W. Willers. "Okay, Beauchamp," Davis said, "You can go in. Good luck."

Michael knocked and opened the door. It was a narrow office, Willers was sitting at his desk with his back to the window, which saw out on a wide expanse of sea. After the somber corridors it was blinding, making it hard to distinguish the expression on Willers's face. Was it proper to come to attention in a monk's robe? No, it would be idiotic, Michael decided. He stood still and said, "Sir."

"Good day. I am lieutenant-Commander Willers. And you are—"

"Sergeant Michael Beauchamp, Seven Troop, Four Commando."

Willers looked at the paper on his desk. "You have no identification at all?"

"I lost my disks, sir, somewhere along the line. I was taken prisoner on March 3, during a reconnaissance on the St. Nazaire coast. I escaped from Stalag Four near Stuttgart in May."

"Seven Troop, Four Commando," Willers repeated. "What

was the name of your seagull, sergeant?" That was meant to be a trick question, a very simple one, though. "Seagull" was the code name for the 2IC, the second in command.

"Captain Dawson, sir."

"Right. Well, we go by the rule book here as we have to in a garrison, and I must get clearance from London, but I'll say you are who you say you are. London also assigns the priorities in air passage but you won't have to wait long. We'll get you back into the fight quickly, I dare say. Are you Canadian, Beauchamp?"

"No, sir. I'm from the U.S., from Philadelphia."

"I see," Willers said with a marked lack of enthusiasm. "You'll need a medical check, do you want it here or can it wait for the UK?"

"It can wait."

"Well, my adjutant will take care of you. You'll find him four doors down."

"Thank you, sir." Michael did not leave.

"Yes. What else, Beauchamp?"

"The lady. My travel companion."

"Ah yes," Willers said slowly. "I understand she was released from hospital recently. She seems to be a very forceful young woman, or so I'm told. She certainly saw to it that no time was wasted getting you out of your Spanish jail." Willers smiled somewhat sourly.

"Eh—could I—" Michael stopped himself. "Thank you, sir."

"She presents me with a bit of a problem, sergeant. We have no space for civilian refugees on the rock."

"I'm sure she'll want to enlist, sir. She is very tough. I don't think either of us would have made it here alone."

"Quite," Willers said. He paused, ticking with his pencil against his teeth. "She's not just a girlfriend you picked up on the way, is she, sergeant?"

Michael had never made his peace with that patronizing edge, that touch of class arrogance, found at the time in any conversation of a British officer with an Other Rank. (In the Commandos it was less obvious, but it was there, too.) It sounded paradoxical but he himself understood very well: this was one of the reasons why he had not put himself up for a commission. Now, he did not answer Willers's question. He held himself rigid and only said, "Sir." Straight out of "Bengal Lancers."

"All right, sergeant. We'll see what we can do."

After that he was back in the corridor, still in his smelly friar's habit, and without so much as a thank you, well done, Michael thought. "You won't have to wait long to get back into the fight." Well, ain't that nice. Thanks loads, lieutenant-commander. Maybe I don't want to hurry all that much to get back into any fucking fights. In the meantime, why don't you get off your ass and into the fight yourself. I'm no hero but I've not been absent for a year with a case of chickenpox. From Stuttgart to Gibraltar I was under a death sentence from the fucking Fuhrer, lieutenant-commander Willers.

Behind him a door opened and an army NCO came out. "Beauchamp?" he asked.

"Yes. Here."

"Why are you standing there in the dark, man? Come in. I have all sorts of treats for you. Foremost, a room all by yourself, you'll be glad to know. I hear you lost your entire kit and we'll start afresh." He looked closely at Michael and began to laugh. "A bath first? Follow me."

"Do you have a Mary de Jongh here from Holland?" Michael asked him.

"Do we ever. She's the heroine of the sergeants' mess. We know all about you two. If it hadn't been for her, you might have spent another year in that robe. She drove them crazy, the intelligence fellows here, I mean. They're a very relaxed group. 'Let's discuss this later, my dear, first taste this excellent sherry.' That kind of thing."

Michael's best moment that day came when he lowered himself slowly into a hot bath. That was uncomplicated bliss. To get back into an anonymous battle dress, woolen socks, and ill-fitting heavy shoes wasn't all that great, although it was nice to roll up the monk's habit and stuff it into a trash can. After his bath he went for a walk, just up and down the street outside looking into the windows of the little shops, Boots, W.H. Smith, everything like High Street in an English town. He was nervous about going into the sergeants' mess, but when the various church clocks started striking six, he thought he'd better get it over with.

And it was okay, everyone came to shake hands with him and say, "Well done," or words to that effect, which was more than Willers had done, and he was at the receiving end of a non-stop round of beers.

And then Marie had come in and he had gone up to her, and they hugged. She looked fine, he thought. A haunted expression which had always, he realized, been just below the surface, had vanished from her face. She is free now, out from under the Germans with their J stamps. I was under death sentence, too, but it was different, mine was still an adventure, a challenge as of famous escapes in history—the stamps the German put on their chosen victims say, you're not our enemy, you are nothing, *Nichts*. Which is precisely what their word *vernichten* (destroy) means. He took a deep breath. "Let's go outside, Mary, let's go for a walk by ourselves," he said.

"Oh, Michael, we can't. It would be very unfriendly, you're the guest of honor here tonight."

And so he was afloat in Guinesses until Marie saw that he began to look faint and said she'd walk him to his room as he was clearly bushed. She kissed him at the door, on his cheek, and he stumbled in and lay down without even turning the light on, got his lumpy shoes off, and passed out cold.

HE WOKE UP from the sound of an explosion. I must have dreamt it, he thought, but then there was another one. Loud yet muffled at the same time, such as he had never heard before. Some new kind of German bomb, he wondered, and he realized he was afraid.

Have I lost it? he asked the pitch-dark, windowless, little room.

He sat up, took his clothes off, and crept under the sheet. Think of it, last night I was lying on a filthy, prickly sack of straw, and now I'm between cool sheets. I should be as happy as Larry. But—

But, I'm back in the fucking war. Courage—it's not a word I've ever heard spoken in earnest by one of the Troop. It's like discipline and patriotism and marching to the whistle of a heroic officer, bayonets at the thirty degree angle—we have dropped those words for good, they had become bullshit. What we will say in earnest is, hey guys, it's hopeless. But I guess we say it as an insurance policy and hope differently. And we believe in individuality, if only from a white scarf or whatever is easily put wrong on a uniform, and we believe in invulnerability almost. No solidarity with outsiders, let alone with an enemy doing-its-duty, you must be joking, contempt, contempt for the Germans and for most everyone else too.

It adds up to a reality, part knowingly childish like the white scarves, part almost beyond death, you might say.

Within that reality I was never scared—or was I? No. It took care of the whole show, tearing your hands on the barbed wire in silence, stealing food and clothes, the peasant corporals of the *Feldgendarmerie*, everything, including the Lieutenant-Commander who did me a favor by omitting any "well done, old fellow" crap when you consider it carefully.

Where you lose your guts, at least I did, is when you are alone, solitary, in that filthy Spanish prison cell. Courage, excuse the word, if it means anything, it is a solitary business, like a spy in an enemy country or those Resistance guys in France. The other thing is vanity or fear of looking ridiculous.

Did that fucking cell undo me? It shouldn't, it mustn't. Didn't I think I might be sharing it with Michel, grand-père Michel. Then it's already solitary for two.

The explosions continued but he went back to sleep. The following day he was told that it was British depth charges he had heard. They were set off every night under water in the bay to protect the ships against enemy submarines sneaking in.

34

MICHAEL HAD EXPECTED TO HUDDLE WITH MARY AND talk for hours about what had happened to them. They would finally look back from Gibraltar to the Santa Lucia and puzzle at its mystery and commemorate grandfather Michel in some sort of way. Michael often thought of Anne and Michel both—but after that first evening he would never again bring up Michel with Mary. He was afraid she'd think he was doing it to make her feel obliged to him.

When he saw her that first night in the mess, wreck as he was, he had been overcome with the desire of their hotel room in Narbonne. It had lasted only a moment. Her first words had ended it. He had also thought that she might need his help with the Gibraltar bureaucracy, but that did not come about, either.

During the day Marie worked as a volunteer at the Women of Gibraltar Support and their evenings in the mess ended with a friendly kiss at the door of her dormitory. "Can't we be alone a bit tomorrow?" he had asked the second night. And she had answered, "You've saved me, don't think I'd ever forget that," which was of course no answer.

She had applied for enlistment in the Wrens, the Women's Royal Naval Service, she told him, and she had had her interview. Now it was a matter of being vetted. She had also shown him her thigh with its six-inch scar, but that was the most he got to see from her body. Perhaps she felt her chance for enlistment could be ruined if she was seen as his little girlfriend; he hoped that was her reason. Meanwhile, he had to do more waiting.

He had received an advance on his back pay and he spent it in the shabbiest bars of Gibraltar. He got a kick out of sitting at the one little table outside a joint called La Passionaria which had a printed British Army notice in the window, "Out of Bounds to all Ranks." Fuck 'em. And he stared at the passing army and navy officers while holding his glass, assuredly not of sherry but of a sickly green pastis. Usually that made them look away. There was some satisfaction in that.

Several women used to wander up and down near that bar, the kind his father would have called "ladies of the night." They weren't quite that; what with the Gibraltar black-out and the curfew for military personnel, they worked from six P.M. (year-round double British summertime) until nine P.M. only and not a minute longer. They killed time looking in shop windows, checked their watches as if waiting for a delayed friend, and in general were as discreet as if they were working the street in a British market town, which was the proper label for Gibraltar anyway if you left out the guns.

Michael was torn between a very indiscriminate lust which hit him in waves, and his longing for Mary and a slowly vanishing hope of the surprise night she could have in store for him. A handsome woman with black hair and dressed like a stage gypsy in "Carmen" broke his resistance the second time he saw her. But once he stood facing her in a little hotel bedroom he didn't dare go on. Suppose he showed up at

Mary's with a dose (as they called it in his army)? "By hand please," he asked hoarsely. And back out on High Street, packed with eager "blokes" and red-faced staff officers, cafés with blaring Spanish orchestras, little shops with copies of "Country Life" in the window, he felt heavy with frustration and a kind of loathing for himself.

All in all those were bad days. And the evenings weren't any better, with the sergeants making passes at Marie which she laughed off, and with her treating him as a "chum" as she called it. This Gibraltar he had thought of as a besieged haven, seemed out of place at the Mediterranean in its coziness of lukewarm beer and cups of tea. One day he suddenly felt overcome with a crippling tiredness, he just made it back to his room where he lay motionless on his bed for he didn't know how long. Then it passed. It's all in the mind, he thought, it's the anti-climax of this place which brings out the accumulated weariness of a year.

One evening he came upon a movie house. The moment he saw it, he knew he had to go there immediately, never mind dinner or curfew. He hadn't known there was a cinema in town, a refuge from all his frustrations and doubts. There was a photograph in a glass case of a couple dancing, nobody less than Fred Astaire and Ginger Rogers as far as he could make out in the dusk (no lights outside a cinema during the black-out). The name of the show was "Chistera" and a passing British Indian policeman told him "chistera" was Spanish for the baskets that catchers use in jai alai. Fred Astaire playing jai alai? Never mind, he would have gone in no matter what.

But it was an American movie and it was Fred Astaire and Ginger Rogers, in "Top Hat." He saw the second half and then the whole thing again. It was dubbed in Spanish but he did not mind, for the songs weren't dubbed and that was what mattered. The way Ginger Rogers sang the word "baby" made him shiver. Afterward, the cashier informed him that Chistera was also Spanish for a top hat, or topèt as she called it.

When those two were dancing in the pavilion in the rain, he loved his country, America, more than he ever had. He was drowning in homesickness or maybe it was nostalgia for his own childhood in what now seemed to have been such a *guileless* world. He saw himself on a hot summer's day in Philadelphia, the high school picnic in Fairmount Park, the girls with their long, tanned, legs dancing with one another to the record player they had brought—maybe they had precisely been playing, "Isn't this a lovely day to be caught in the rain."

He wandered off in a welter of thoughts and feelings. It was a Saturday night, there was a press of people in the dark streets of the old town with only here and there a street lamp, its light bulb painted blue. But he was oblivious to the crowd. Even his plan to try and lure Mary into bed that evening had been forgotten. He didn't think about the war nor about the curfew. The only emotion he felt was in his tie with that film and its music, its simplicity, its untiredness as he felt it, and Ginger Rogers.

His London clearance came unexpectedly, the very next morning, as one paragraph in a long service message. At seven o'clock the adjutant himself came to his room to wake him up and tell him he had to get ready in ten minutes, there was a space for him on the eight o'clock Sunderland flying boat. He scribbled a note to Marie and the adjutant promised he'd give it to her that very evening without fail.

The plane had no separate seats but, like most transport

planes at the time, benches along each side. Over the shoulder of the man opposite him he caught his last glance of Algeciras Bay and its radiant blue under the early morning sun.

Michael, in 1941

35

Looking around him, Michael discovered the plane was a democratic mix; from where he sat he could see a sergeant, two privates, two lieutenants, a captain, and even a major. Next to him sat a second lieutenant with Royal Artillery shoulder badges, smoking a black cigarette. When he noticed Michael looking at it, he told him, "Turkish, sergeant, and exceptionally nice. They're smuggled into Cairo. Like to try one?" and he held out his case.

"Thank you," Michael said, deciding just then not to call anyone "sir" on this flight. The Gibraltar adjutant had seen to it that someone had sewn sergeant stripes on his jacket, although he would just as well have done without. But he had no shoulder tabs, a non-fitting cap, his battle dress was too tight and its color, from many washings, was a khaki bordering on dirty yellow. All in all, an unimpressive anonymity.

"Excellent," Michael said, inhaling with great pleasure.

"Aren't they? I'll have a hard time getting used to Woodbines again. Have you been out of England long?"

"Yes. Quite a while."

"Me too. I wonder how things have changed. Whiskey is now weighed against gold, I've been assured."

"Maybe that just shows nobody has much use for gold any more."

The lieutenant laughed. "I didn't think of it that way. But talking about whiskey—" He unzipped the bag he had between his feet and brought out a flask. He poured some of its contents into the silver cap and offered it to Michael, who hesitated.

"Seen from a plane, the sun is always below the yardarm," the lieutenant said. "Drink up."

Michael lifted the cap but just then the plane lurched violently and dove into the cloud blanket they had been flying over. "Jesus," the lieutenant said, "what's going on?"

Up front in the flying boat an argument was in progress. Eventually one of the crew came down the center aisle. "A German, an ME 110," he informed his passengers. "Our captain saw him before he saw us, or so we think. We're all right now." The plane was flying in the clouds; after the sharp sunlight its cabin was half-dark.

"I spilled your precious whiskey," Michael said.

"Here's a refill." The lieutenant looked somewhat shaken and he took a long draft from the flask before filling Michael's cup.

Michael leaned back, he could feel the vibration of the plane against his body. He was dizzy. It's the whiskey on an empty stomach, he decided. The lieutenant beside him now sat staring ahead; on his other side an NCO was asleep, his mouth open.

It was odd to be back in this all-male world with its precise and limited scope and its intimacy with dying. But nowadays the same holds true for half the world. I'll think about it later, when we're in England, in a couple of hours, lots of cold, fresh, air. But he began to feel the same leaden tiredness that had struck him some days before. I must snap out of it, he thought, I'll go wash my face with cold water.

When he stood up, he felt so wobbly that he had to sit down again. He became aware of sweat dripping down his face. Dammit, what is the matter with me, he thought.

Presently, he fell into a doze.

The flying boat set down with a series of shocks. Michael opened his eyes and saw gray, choppy water. "The Solent," his neighbor said. "We made it."

"One more time."

"Yes. One more time."

The plane emptied quickly and when a crew member walked down the aisle, he saw Michael still sitting there, hunched up and shivering.

"Everybody off, sergeant."

Michael produced a smile. "I don't seem to be able to stand up," he muttered.

An ambulance was called and then he found himself on a gurney in a hospital corridor without knowing how he had gotten there.

"Where did they take me?" he whispered to a nurse who bent over him.

"Portsmouth General Hospital," she said cheerfully. "Open wide."

She popped a thermometer into his mouth. When she came back to look at it, she made a face. The mercury stood at 103.8.

"Well?" Michael whispered.

"Never you mind. We'll take care of you."

Later that day they diagnosed typhoid fever.

Marie, in 1941

36

The Gibraltar adjutant had put Michael's note to Marie in the breast pocket of his battle dress with the intention of giving it to her after dinner. He remembered it as he was smoking his last cigarette in the officer's reading room and he immediately went to the sergeant's mess where she could be found evenings, Michael had told him. But she wasn't there and he left the note with the barkeeper who put it in his till under the liquor vouchers and forgot about it.

After work that day, Marie had found an "On His Majesty's Service" re-use yellow envelope on her dormitory bunk. She read that she had been accepted in the Women's Royal Navy Service. She would be on the next five-weeks training course at Gibraltar, starting in two days time. After it she would receive "a more definite posting."

She sat on her cot, waving the note typed on flimsy yellow paper, and crying, "Ha! Ha!" with tears of happiness running down her cheeks. "I will get you, mister 'itler," she said. Only now did she feel truly freed.

She jumped up and went to look for Michael who had to be told. She would explain to him why she had felt she must wait for this and hold anything personal in abeyance. But when she got to his room, its door stood open and a soldier was making up the bed with fresh sheets.

"Do you know where Sergeant Beauchamp is?" she asked him.

"He had this room didn't he? He was off this morning, back to England, and I got the room, the quartermaster had promised me. But who are you?"

Marie, wearing the borrowed uniform of a nurse's aide under a man's battle dress jacket for warmth, was a somewhat unorthodox sight. "Never mind that," she answered.

She went back to the dormitory and lay down on her bunk, still holding her letter. Sad, she thought, but I won't let it spoil this day. It's my fault, but it seemed so wrong, so cheap, to get out from under the Germans and celebrate that, so to speak, by jumping in bed with the first British soldier—but of course that's not how it was. It was Michael, it wasn't "a soldier."

It was that damn officer, that Willers bastard who interrogated me, he made it all cheap and dubious, he froze me. Did the sergeant pick you up, miss, or did you pick him up? That was what he was really asking in that posh Oxford voice. Had you been active in the local resistance, miss? No? Why exactly were you on the run? Are you, eh, of the Hebrew persuasion? Well, fuck you, Captain Willers or whatever the fuck you are. I'll be in uniform two days from now and then you will never again have the chance to call me "miss" in that peculiar tone of voice you used for the occasion, and I'll manage not to see you and not to salute you, and maybe one day I'll get the chance to trip you up right into the sea.

But you should have understood, Michael, what I was about.

She thought of her mother hiding on that farm in Zeeland. Don't let them get you down, mam. You're not hiding because you are scared of them, you are at war with them. Consider yourself a guerilla.

But she saw a bunch of German soldiers led by their *Gefreiter*, on bicycles maybe, circling along the dikes of those flat polders, visible from a mile away, with their dull faces and their fat asses and their rifles—Gibt es unterduykers here?—and poking in the hay lofts and looking in closets and attics. Trying it out on some halfwit farm laborer, Hey, you, Pete, come here, there's a hundred guilders for you if you can tell us who may be hiding Jews around here—

Once I'm in uniform, she thought, when I'm a Wren or an apprentice Wren or whatever, I'll go see the paymaster and ask him about Michael. There must be an armed forces mailing address in England I can write to. In the fullness of time he'll get it. And maybe when they post me to England, I'll find him and we'll have a date and won't he look up seeing me on His Majesty's Service. That's all I need to be happy about him: if we have one cup of tea, and he sees me just once, his equal, and he'll know he did the right thing and I wasn't just a waste of his time.

And the Wrens must have officers, mustn't they, maybe I'll be one, and I'll smile at him and say, "You don't have to salute me, Michael, but only because you bluffed me past that Vichy Nazi cop."

Marie wrote her letter. It finally was returned to the Gibraltar post office, stamped, "Not now in an active service unit." But by that time Marie had already been posted in England.

Michael, in 1942

37

It was several weeks before they brought Michael his first solid food. Well, solid—it was a soft-boiled egg. "I hate those," he muttered, but he had to eat it.

Later that day an army doctor came to talk to him. "You are going to have a lengthy recovery, sergeant," he said, "physical therapy, and so on. Some months." He pulled up one of Michael's legs. "Look at that, it's just a stick." He had a thin smile. "Don't worry, the war won't be over. It'll be hard work, but you can do it."

"Yes."

The doctor studied the chart. "Where did I catch this, sir?" Michael asked him.

"Who knows. Dirty water, in Spain presumably. Look at your fever graph, here you were near 105 degrees, it was touch and go, and we thought we were going to lose you."

Michael looked at that landscape of sharp peaks and turned his head away. "I'd rather not study that, doc. It gives me the willies."

"The willies," the doctor repeated. "Do you know that your country has joined the war?"

"No kidding. On which side?"

The doctor stared at him and then decided this had been a joke. "Would you want to consider a transfer to the American forces, sergeant? We can get you someone who knows about those things to come and see you."

"No such luck, doctor. You got me as good as new and you'll have to return me as good as new. Can't get rid of me now."

The doctor had another thin smile and left with a wave of his hand.

"We patients have a hard time," Michael told the nurse, "trying to keep our doctors' spirits up."

HIS NEXT VISITOR was an army vicar. Those men never brought up religion unless a patient showed a desire for it; Michael's vicar brought him a candy bar (which the nurse took away) and a novel, "Captain Hornblower." He asked him if he had any letters he wanted to dictate for parents or friends.

"I only write them about my ups," Michael said, "not about my downs."

"But that's precisely when you need them, sergeant."

"Please call me Beauchamp, sir. I am not defined by my being a sergeant."

"Yes, I can see that," the vicar answered. "So for now, I'll bid you goodbye."

"Oh. Wait, vicar, please. I'm sorry, I was getting out of hand. There is someone who should hear from me, and they've forbidden me to sit up."

"Of course, Beauchamp," the vicar said, mildly accentuating the name. He brought out a pad and pencil. "Go ahead."

"It is addressed to Marie de Jongh, that's with g-h. Women's

Royal Navy service, Gibraltar. Is that enough of an address?"

"There's a postal code but my office will take care of that."

"Good. Here goes. 'Dear Mary'." He paused. He remembered how he had told her on that Montpellier café terrace that he had put C of E as his religion to get a nice funeral with music. I got close. But it wouldn't have bothered her much, it would seem.

"Yes?" asked the vicar.

"Oh, sorry, vicar. Can we just say, 'Dear Mary'? And then sign, 'Michael Beauchamp, Portsmouth General Hospital'?"

"Consider it done, as you say in the States," the vicar said. "Take care of yourself, young man."

His departure left Michael with a fever again, but not unhappily so. Odd as it must sound, there was something cheerful about being a sick soldier in an English wartime hospital. The nurses were nice and most of them were very pretty, too—or maybe any woman's face would look pretty in contrast to the jowls of one's smelly fellow servicemen. It's a sensual pleasure, he thought, lying here and stretching your body and having nothing to do, no getting up at dawn, nothing to be responsible for.

Even with a splitting headache.

He closed his eyes and tried to think of Mary. Perhaps typhoid makes you impotent, he thought, I read that once. I must test it as soon as I feel up to it. Just by hand.

Although a soldier's service record was kept confidential in hospital, there had been enough rumors about Michael's escape to make him one of the celebrities of the ward. An auxiliary nurse went so far as to ask him for his signature in her daybook, but she was very young. He was taken off intravenous feeding and when his headaches lessened he was allowed to walk to the toilet by himself, which he considered a great blessing.

And then one morning he was told he could read a book, but not for longer than an hour at the time. He started with the vicar's (and C.S. Forester's) "Captain Hornblower." Michael was born near the sea, as was his father, and grandfather Michel, and was as captivated by it as they had been. After an hour of those scrubbed decks and wind and water, and the Captain who had too much imagination to be precisely brave but who stayed *calm*, he felt a new man. He convinced the nurse to let him go on reading and he spent the rest of that day finishing the book. When his nurse came back, he was on the last page and she waited for that. Then she popped the thermometer in his mouth and found that his fever had gone.

"The sea did that," he said.

Once he could sit up in a chair without getting his fever back, they started sending him to the physical therapy center a couple of blocks away from the hospital. The first time he was awkward, staying close to the houses, and as soon as his time was up at the center, hastening back to his hospital bed. That was because of the picture in his mind of those fever peaks close to the red line marked "fatal" (that was his imagination, there was no such line on the chart). Eventually his legs began to feel normal and he started looking around on the street. He took detours to the harbor, badly damaged by the German bombs of the past two years, but filled with turbulent activity. He sat there whenever it wasn't raining and watched the picketboats darting around against the gray silhouettes of the great warships anchored farther out. He was spellbound by those slick gray and gray-blue ships under their red, white, and blue flags, and their neat guns. Here, he imagined, was a clean and glamorous way to wage war, traditional and hyper-modern at the same time. You'd feel stronger, more ensconced, than in the infantry and more part of a team than a fighter pilot ever was. Wish I had gone for the navy. But then, it is such an English thing, I might have been an unhappy oddity. Better off among the commando mongrels.

An orderly came to the hospital ward and brought him a new battle dress, one that fit, with commando tabs and a beret that almost fit, the whole, the nurses agreed, very smart. Dressed in that outfit, he decided to go and have tea after his therapy treatment, in a posh tearoom on the High Street he had passed every day (he wasn't allowed alcohol).

Most of the customers were women and it was disappointing that no one in the tearoom showed interest in his entry. He took a small table near a window, tucked his beret under a shoulder-strap, and took his time lighting a cigarette. This is more like it, he thought.

He looked out on the busy street, the sun broke through for a moment, and it made a nice scene in spite of all the bomb ruins, many men and women in uniform, also shoppers, lots of baby carriages. The houses right across from the tearoom had been hit and lost their facade but the site had been neatened up a bit with newly planted bushes, and some of the exposed rooms were kept dry with a huge banner, "Quiet nights thanks to Russia." There had been only one raid on Portsmouth since he was there, and Russia, which the experts had given three to six weeks, was still in there (although the experts had not taken that as their cue to shut up a bit).

There was such an intensity in that bombed street outside

his window, as in the life of the port all over— It sounds crazy, he said to himself, but one day some of those people out there, and I myself if I'm still around, may look back on this and may well think those were the best days of our lives.

He kept going to the tearoom after PT. One afternoon there, he became aware of a very animated conversation at the table behind him, many young women's voices, much laughing, and when he peeked over his shoulder he saw a group of Wrens sitting there and one was looking straight at him. He sloshed his tea over his new uniform trousers: he was looking Marie in the face.

She opened her mouth but made no sound; she blushed fiercely. The she stood up, walked around her friends, bent over Michael and kissed him on his cheek.

Later they walked along the waterfront together. They held hands for a moment but then they had to salute a staff officer and they didn't get back to it.

Michael broke the long silence. "Bloody hell, it's almost six. I've to report back to the hospital."

"I'll walk you there. We're free till eight."

"Where do you have to be?" So far they had avoided personal questions.

"I'm stationed at Warsash. Today was my first time off base; we got leave to buy stuff for ourselves in Portsmouth. At twenty-hun—at eight o'clock, the bus takes us back to the base. It's only fifteen minutes."

"Warsash. I never heard that name."

"It's tiny. But with lots of picket boats. It is on the estuary of the Hamble. We work very hard."

He laughed. "You've sure become acclimated. You sound like a veteran sailor, Mary. And you look like one."

She made a face. "It's serious, Michael. You must take me serious."

"Oh but I do. I do! You look splendid. Waging war becomes you."

That made her smile.

"That was a great day, Michael, when I got the notice that they'd take me in the WRNS; you can't understand, it was my manumission."

"I do understand."

"I ran all over the place, all those endless corridors of Gibraltar, to find you and tell you, but wouldn't you know, that same fucking morning you had taken off."

"I—"

"And you know what my first thought was? To see you again. In my Wren uniform, and to make you feel you hadn't wasted your time and it had all been worthwhile."

He smiled at her, a happier smile than she had seen from him so far. "Dear Mary. It was all worthwhile. I knew that already before seeing you in the bloomin' King's services."

"And here you were at death's door ten miles away from me. If all our letters hadn't gone wonky, I'd have been sitting at your bedside and brought you grapes weeks ago."

"I don't think you'd have found any grapes in Portsmouth."

"I'd have gone straight to the Director of Naval Ordnance. 'Sir, we need grapes for the hero of the battle of Santa Lucia.' He'd never have dared say that he hadn't heard of that battle."

And so she might have, he thought.

They had come to the entrance gate of the hospital, and stood across from the guardpost which was still fortified with sandbags. The guard came out of his hut and said, "Sergeant, you can't stay there. In or out. We're closing the gate."

Michael took a long look at her, from her shoes to her hat. "We've reversed roles," he said. "And I don't mind a bit. You may be my commanding officer."

"Good night, Michael. Take care."

"Will you let me know when you have time off next?"

She pulled his head toward her and kissed his mouth. "Yes, I will. I will indeed."

Michael, in 1941

38

He hurried back to his ward, undressed behind the screen, and crawled into bed. Just in time. The hospital worker was wheeling in the cart with the evening meal trays. "Sit up, sarge," she said.

"I'm a wreck." Michael put his pillow upright and leaned against it. "I'm not hungry."

"Tut, tut. Mutton stew. That's a week's rations there on your plate. You chaps don't know how lucky you are."

Bloody hell, as we say here. We do know. But all my training, a year of running and climbing, down the drain. Look at my arms, it's pathetic. Will I ever get back there?

Think what Mary must have thought, seeing me like this. I talked about reversed roles. And how we reversed roles! Here I was this tough guy, coming to the aid of this poor Dutch girl in tears, Jewish refugee girl, I'll get you out of here, dear, nothing to it for a commando. And here we are in England and she's metamorphosed into a bloody smart Wren rating who now speaks the King's English without an atom of Dutch accent and who was about to call eight o'clock "Twenty hundred hours" but corrected herself in time, in case this poor emaciated slob with his old-age pensioners' shuffle didn't understand. Fucking hell, Michael.

His stew was cold and greasy but now he decided he'd better eat it.

He thought a lot about her in the following days, trying to understand how he felt, and trying to guess how she felt about him. He tried out a speech, "Mary, I don't know if I love you but I know I need you to get back on my feet, and you may well ask, 'What do I get out of that?' I've no answer to that, but if somehow you yourself have an answer we'll live happily ever after or at least till they think I'm ready for another weekend excursion to a French bathing resort—"

But as time went by and he didn't hear from her, he stopped his speculations. He concentrated on his recalcitrant body and worked twice as long in the PT center as they required of him.

But there were nights when he woke up in the dark ward with its blacked-out windows and just one blinking little light over the door opening, and felt totally abandoned, no one on either side of the ocean giving a good goddamn whether he was dead or alive. Well, maybe my mom. Then Mary seemed the only lifebelt to cling to—for no other reason, he thought bitterly, than that she has a cunt, that we can screw, the only real contact between two human beings in this desolate world.

It was raining hard. Michael came out of the PT center and stood in its doorway, looking at the passers-by huddled under umbrellas, the trucks and jeeps splashing by, the rain falling with such force that the drops made bubbles where they landed in the gutters. A childhood memory, waiting with his mother in the doorway of a store for the rain to let up. "When rain makes bubbles," she had told him, "it signifies that the rain will stop soon."

He saw a woman in blue across the haze of water, under an

awning at the opposite side of the street. He wiped his face and looked again. Mary, in her blue uniform. She waved at him and he crossed the street on the run, dodging a Bedford truck. He thought, the first time I'm running again.

They went into a pub and sat in the windowsill with their ginger ales. Michael studied her face. How terrific she looks. I surely don't rate a woman like that anymore.

"I have a surprise for you," Marie said.

"Grapes."

"Close your eyes. All right. You can look."

He opened his eyes. She held her hand out toward him, and in her palm lay a Chubb house key.

"My God," he muttered.

"Indeed, Michael. Nothing less than divine interference in our fates."

"Your fate, too?"

"My fate, too."

THEY FELL into each other's arms without an atom of awkwardness, but it did not become a repeat of their French hotel room days. His pleasure in his own body had gone and he had to hang on by his nails (so to speak) to even make it. She didn't comment though, she gave him a peck on his cheek, jumped up and started to paddle through the apartment in the nude, touching little plastic elephants "for good luck" and looking at the books and the pictures on the walls. She boiled water to make tea. Michael watched her from the daybed.

She was sitting on a stool at the kitchen counter, she had her feet tucked under the rung of the stool, her bottom just rested on it. He stared at the curve of her thigh, the soft dent made by the edge of the wood, and in that instant a wave of genuine desire swept over him. She turned toward him and said, "Come get your tea," but when she saw the expression on his face, she smiled, anxiously almost. She got off her stool and came over to him, she kneeled on the bed between his legs and very slowly let herself down on him. He held her tight and rolled over with her.

Afterward they lay still for a long time. "Nice," she said in a light voice.

You bring me back to life, he thought. "This is what the doctor ordered," he told her.

"Well, thanks a heap. Tell him I'm not a volunteer nurse's aide."

He shook his head. "I'm just trying out my American matter-of-factness. I'm just bull-shitting. I love you, Mary."

"Worse and worse. Stop gabbing, Michael, and kiss me."

He pressed his mouth on hers but she shook her head free. "Not there, Michael. Here. Get serious."

He was called before the medical board and asked if he felt fit for active service, and he answered, yes.

"We'll do another week of physical therapy," the chairman, an RAMC captain, said. "In the meantime your new posting and your rail warrant will reach you at Portsmouth General. And for heaven's sake, man, eat more. If the Germans capture you, they'll announce there's famine in England."

Three days later they brought Michael his posting form with his breakfast tray. It was to a place called Harlech on the coast of North Wales. He made his way to the only phone booth on the floor with a fistful of change, and tried to place a call to the Wren station at Warsash. He didn't succeed: "The circuits are busy," the operator said, "only military priority calls."

Dammit, and only three days left.

In the bed next to him was a transport sergeant, a pretty rough type it seemed, whose friends smuggled whiskey in for him and cheered him up with stories about the girls who came for evening drives with them into the countryside.

Michael got to eat his dinner in a chair by the window, and when two friends of the transport sergeant showed up, he went over to them. "Fellows, I am in a real emergency situation."

"Eh?"

"They're about to dismiss me from here and send me off to North Wales. And there's my girl here, I have to see her."

The men looked at him now with more sympathy.

"You're here with a light truck, right?" he asked. "Could I borrow it for an hour, an hour and a half at most?"

They looked at their friend in bed. "Should we?"

"Yeah—he's all right."

"Okay then. She's not in the hospital parking lot, of course. On the corner, at the dentist office. The plate says ATC 679. We padlock the steering wheel, here's the key. We call her a lorry."

A 27, the road to Fareham. Michael had looked it up. Left turn on the A 27. He was in such a hurry, he dropped the key on the floor of the truck and had to grope for it amidst cigarette stubs and other, indefinable, objects. Through Fareham. And there was the signpost, Warsash, 3.4 miles.

It was rapidly getting dark. A barrier loomed up with barbed wire and a sign, "Naval Personnel Only." He parked the truck in a lay-by and continued on foot. No one paid any attention to him.

The road turned at the Southampton river, its water was glimmering under the last daylight, buildings showed up with pinpoints of blue lights. He went up to the water's edge and came to a house with a large terrace fronting the estuary. Marie had told him about that terrace, they called it the quarterdeck, for everything here was named in nautical terms. A woman and a man were standing at the railing of the terrace, looking out over the river. He saw them from the back, the light was fading, but he recognized the woman as Mary, without the slightest doubt. He was about to call when she turned toward the man beside her and put her arms around him, and they kissed.

Michael stood motionless, blinked, and then ran back to his truck thinking only, she must not see me.

"TOMORROW, MICHAEL, is your big day then," the night nurse said.

"Yes—I'll miss you all. Specially you. I don't even know your name."

"Ellen." She kissed him on his forehead. "The best of Irish luck, as we say in my family."

It was the end of his last day in Portsmouth General. The following morning he was to be driven to the station with his kit, all new stuff, for the train journey to Harlech on the Irish Sea, or more precisely, on Cardigan Bay, where there was a commando base.

"May I have a sleeping pill?" he asked the nurse.

"For sure. Are you nervous?"

"Sad."

She gave him a long look but asked no further questions.

I've lost my sense of perspective, he thought. I'm going back to this big fat war and I'm moping about a girl of nineteen or twenty. But I would have liked to make her the love of my life. Or of the war. Or of the year. I'm tired of myself. The hell with it. Let's just get on with it and those of us who make it, can go home, until the fucking Germans try a third time, anyway.

He had gotten two sleeping pills from Ellen and they had to shake him the next morning to wake him up. "How do you feel, sergeant?"

"Lousy. I have a taste in my mouth of old bicycle tires."

He sat in the windowsill with his breakfast tray. It's true. I will miss this place. How we hang on to any little familiar hole to crawl into. Pathetic.

A THREE-TON BEDFORD was parked at the main entrance. The guard at the door pointed it out with his thumb. "He's taking you to the station. You're the commando with typhus, right?"

"In a manner of speaking. That big brute of a truck for one man? What a waste."

"Don't worry your head about that, sergeant. He's collecting supplies for us at the freight yard."

"So where is he?"

"He'll be down. Just rest your feet in the cabin."

Michael had a long wait before the driver showed up. "Sorry, mate," he said. "Papers. You'll make your train. Wind down your window, will you? I'm boiling."

They drove off, but the driver had to come to a screeching halt at the gate where a long line of children suddenly started to cross.

"Look at that pretty teacher," he said. He stuck his head out the window. "Hey, love, you are sabotaging the war effort."

"Michael!" a voice sounded at the other side of the truck. He started. There was Marie standing beside his window, smiling in the clear morning, a blush on her face. She had been running.

"I phoned," she said, "and heard you're off today! I got a lift, I ran the last part. We must—why do you look so odd at me?"

"Love," the driver said, "we'd like to have a long natter, but this young hero has to catch his train."

"I don't think anything—" Michael began.

"Here, sarge," the driver interrupted, "move up. Your lady can ride to the station with us." He reached past Michael to open the door and Marie climbed in. The truck started off.

"It was nice of you to come and say goodbye," Michael said.

"Think of it!" she cried, "I ran half the way but if that line of children hadn't stopped you, I'd have missed him."

"That's right," the driver answered. He appeared to take a strong interest in the situation. "The hand of fate, I'd say. Makes you think."

"But," Michael began again, "What is the point?"

"You stupid clod!" the driver shouted at an automobilist who tried to cut in on him.

"Two nights ago," Michael said, "I—"

"Now listen, sarge." The driver turned to him. "Don't bite the hand of fate. This young lady ran all the way to see you off. So never mind 'two nights ago.'"

"You just mind the traffic, please," Michael said. "Two nights ago I came to Warsash. To say goodbye."

"And?"

"I found you very occupied."

Marie shook her head. "Oh Michael, come on. That boy? That was Tom."

"And who is he, miss?" the driver asked. "Us two would like to know."

She smiled at him. "You concentrate on the traffic as the sergeant told you. Tom is a very young boy who got word that his older brother was killed in North Africa. We're trying to help him, all of us."

"Mary—I—"

The truck stopped with a squeal. "Attention all day trippers," the driver called out. " Portsmouth railway station. This is your last stop."

Marie opened the door and jumped to the street, and Michael fished his kit out from behind him, shook hands, and got out after her. "Jesus," he said, "I've got two minutes."

"Let's run."

He put the kitbag on his shoulder and together they ran down the hall. They just squeezed through as the platform gate was closing, he threw his kitbag in the door of the first compartment they came to, and climbed on the step. "I'll write you a letter," he told her in a subdued voice.

The train got into motion but she kept up with it for a moment. "I'll write first," she cried. "Believe in me, Michael. Where are you off to?"

For answer he smiled, a weak smile.

"Think what the driver said! The hand of fate, that I got to you."

"I'm in Harlech, in Wales," he called back, but she shook her head at the noise drowning out his voice.

The compartment was empty. He fell down on the bench. Well, he thought, well. He didn't get further than that.

Marie, in 1942

39

Marie, or Mary as Michael thought of her, took a long time to write him that "first letter" she had promised him in Portsmouth station. She knew she wouldn't get away with just forgetting about the Tom incident, and she felt a dislike of explaining it further, of appearing to apologize for something which was none of his business.

When she finally wrote, it became a rather flat letter which she regretted afterward. Anyway, Michael's sour answer got to Warsash only after she had left there, and in the mail office of the base her name, by then, was on the list of those whose correspondence was not to be forwarded but held "until further notice."

Marie had by now become a very different woman indeed from the one Michael had bluffed through the Vichy police check. In an amazingly short time she had traveled the emotional distance from refugee, citizen of a German-occupied and disenfranchised country, to an NCO in an arrogantly superior formation of navy women. She spoke English and French with a hardly noticeable Dutch accent, and she hadn't come to the WRNS from the family home but after an escape through Vichy France and Franco Spain. People began to know about her.

One morning at Warsash she was called to the WRNS director's office and introduced to an elderly civilian. He asked her to tell him about herself and they talked for an hour, and then he invited her to have lunch with him in Portsmouth. They knew him in the restaurant and produced cake for desert with coffee—a habit he had picked up in France, he said. Over the coffee he asked her, looking very casual about it, "Would you be willing to return to the continent on a mission?" Then he said she should take her time thinking it over. Its danger was obvious and no one would think less of her if she didn't do it. In fact, no one at the WRNS except for its director would ever know of it.

The suggestion took Marie's breath away. It was an appalling idea, a return to the murderous, dreary, and desperate streets of occupied Europe. Impossible, she thought, my new life would tumble down around my ears, it would all have been a sham and a pretense lasting a couple of months, and I'd just be a pitiful Jewish refugee again. But then she said to herself, no, to the contrary, maybe it would be a test of the genuineness of my life. I wouldn't be on the run this time. I'd be stronger than they are.

She took a sip of her coffee and looked over her cup at the man. He was watching her reaction with a kind of benevolent curiosity, and she smiled at him.

"Would I be given a pistol?" she suddenly asked.

He seemed surprised.

"You shouldn't think of this as a motion picture adventure, my dear," he answered. "Of course you would be armed, of course you'll receive the best possible training and briefing we can provide. But it is not a little thing, as you know as clearly as I. Think quietly about it."

"I don't have to do it," she said. "It is not a little thing. I will do it. What does it consist of?"

"We want you to be a guide. To guide stranded pilots of ours, and certain others, through France and Spain. Just as you did with sergeant Beauchamp. Except that this time you will have contacts along the line. And those men will be safe once you've got them to our Barcelona consulate. You won't have to depend on a miracle such as the one of the Santa Lucia monastery."

She was shocked. "How do you know about that, sir?"

"Nothing mysterious, my dear. Sergeant Beauchamp wrote a full report about his escape, as he was asked to."

"Of course." She was pondering this. Somehow she had thought of that as her and Michael's secret, private, adventure.

"He didn't dwell much on it," the man told her. "Almost as if he were embarrassed. But he had to mention it, or we wouldn't have understood why you weren't turned back like most of our chaps at that time."

"Did you, and your, eh, colleagues, really think of it as a miracle?"

"I gather the monks did. But no, I think we'd call it an extreme coincidence. Only three of us know about it—it would have made you two quite famous otherwise."

"I wouldn't call it a coincidence, though," Marie said. "I'd call it a concurrence."

He smiled. "A fine distinction. A concurrence not of time but of place. I can see it is clever of us to put our faith in you."

"But I don't think Michael Beauchamp would look on our escape as me guiding him," she said.

"Well, my dear, we both know how vain young men are. No harm in that."

Santa Lucia, as said, had left Michael feeling vulnerable. He felt he hadn't really beaten the odds of an escape from a prison camp; nothing he had done would help someone else escaping. He almost felt as if he had cheated.

Very differently, Marie felt comforted every time she thought about it. Another victim, another good guy of history had joined them there. If it was no miracle, it was nonetheless miraculous.

Michael, in 1942 and 1943

40

When Michael arrived in Harlech, Captain Dawson, the Second-in-Command, called him in, told him he was the only man on that raid who had succeeded escaping, and then announced with a smile that he was putting him up for a commission. To his surprise, Michael declined.

Dawson had expected him to be pleased, if only with the change from noise and lager in the sergeants mess to the peace and the sherry of the officers' reading room. Indeed, Michael would have loved the comforts, some privacy the first one of them, which came with being an officer, but he couldn't imagine himself making decisions which would send this man rather than that one to his death.

There was no choice but to get through this war. But the reason the world found itself in such calamity was precisely that it had been run by what his fellow commandos called "officer chaps." They would have had trouble giving a concise definition of the term but they understood its meaning very precisely.

In Portsmouth Hospital Michael had asked the vicar not to address him as sergeant because being one "didn't define him." Now he became the senior one, one of those NCOs who run the show. The popular image of British commandos at the time was of athletes if not of muscle-bound wild men, but in reality most COs (commanding officers) were more interested in their men's intelligence than in their sturdiness. Dawson used to say, "We're not fighting the Germans with clubs."

This meant that Michael wasn't less important to Seven Troop because of his physical condition (the medical board in Portsmouth had given him a limited clearance only); to the contrary, he was really doing an officer's job of logistics. And yet, those words of his to the vicar remained true. In a sense, he was still playing a role. Being a sergeant, being a soldier, did not define him. He was a tongue-in-cheek soldier in many ways.

Presumably the reason he got away with this was his being the only American in a unit of Englishmen and Welshmen, plus a few Free French in the transport section. He was accepted by them as a man who wasn't aloof, shy maybe, somewhat of an outsider by nature. If early on some had thought him a bit of a sissy because he didn't drink enough beer and didn't use the word fuck often enough, his escape from the Stuttgart Stalag under the menace of Hitler's death sentence had taken care of that.

In his two army years before he became a prisoner-of-war, Michael had led a first-class love life, or sex life would be the better word. There was an ebullience about him in those days that made him very appealing to women. He hadn't lost it in the prison camp and his escape had put him on a new high. But this had now vanished. There were enough young women in and around Harlech who were easy, and for whom these men in their unorthodox outfits had a special glamor. Michael shared in that even if he did little to flaunt it, and thus he too had his occasional tussle in a dark storeroom or on the wet grass. But there was never a spark, the conversation afterward was of the "Are you okay?" and "God, more rain" kind and it made him think of Mary with great misery.

On a rainy Sunday afternoon in Harlech (possibly the zero point on a Fahrenheit scale of social excitement), Michael came upon a shop which, contrary to Welsh doctrine, appeared to be open. It was really a cottage with a sign saying, "Antiques and Things," but just the door being ajar was enough of an enticement to go in. And there, amidst the trinkets and bowls, he found a genuine wind-up phonograph. This will save my sanity, he felt.

It took a while to find the storekeeper, a pleasant-looking woman with an accent that gave him much trouble. After they had ironed out the great British-American phonograph-gramophone word dispute, the machine became his for the sum of twelve shillings. But now he needed records, and the woman declared she had seen a few in her attic recently. He was please to take a seat and wait, and presently she reappeared. "Four!" she announced.

"Wonderful," Michael said. "May I see?'

The first one he looked at was a piano recording of "Highlights of Robert Schumann's Kreisleriana." "Why do you look like that, man?" the storekeeper asked indignantly. "Look here. Pianist Vladimir Horowitz. Is that good enough for the army?"

"Well, yes, of course, but you see, in a sergeants' mess—What are the others?"

The second record was more highlights of "Kreisleriana" and as Michael had begun to fear, so were the last two. Beggers can't be choosers, and he got them all four, at a shilling each. It illustrates Michael being accepted that the sergeants' mess did not revolt. Seven Troop became no doubt the only unit in any army anywhere where the men hummed "Kreisleriana" highlights during their daily tasks.

That was the most memorable event of Michael's year of rain and waiting.

MICHAEL, IN 1944

41

MICHAEL JUMPED FROM THE WEASEL INTO THE VERY cold water of the North Sea. A Weasel is an amphibian armored carrier, running on tracks like a tank. The water came up to his middle and he thought that the shock would stop his heart from beating. But then he managed to get into motion, waded to the shore, climbed over a concrete barrier, and started up a dune.

Halfway to the top he felt drained of all strength; he turned on his back, lay still, and looked up at the gray sky. A hesitant rain started to wet his face. "Keep going, Beauchamp," a man on the beach shouted at him through a megaphone. Somehow he got back on his feet and completed the climb, crawling most of the way.

Seven Troop, Four Commando was in training, practicing the assault on a heavily fortified dune coastline. The coast they were on was Belgian territory, liberated several months after D-Day.

Antwerp, the big port, had been seized by a British armored division, but its harbor (crucial for supplying the armies in the west) was blocked. Across the mouth of Antwerp's access to the sea lies an island, Walcheren, part of the Dutch province of

Zeeland. And this Walcheren was still in the hands of the Germans, in fact some of their best, the Waffen SS. It had been sown with batteries of German guns, everything from rapid-firing 75's to huge 220's, cannon of near 9 inch caliber, heavier than the armament of most warships. Any freighter trying to get past Walcheren to Antwerp would have been sunk in minutes.

Number Four Commando was practicing its assault on the dunes of Ostend and everyone knew the reason: the abandoned German sea defenses of Ostend, and its landscape, resembled Walcheren. It was obvious that they would presently be expected to attack Walcheren and unblock the port of Antwerp.

Ostend was never a really cheerful beach resort. It was too cold for that even in summer, and the Belgians lacked the touch of the French in their resorts farther south. Once, Ostend oysters were shipped in ice-packed railway wagons to St. Petersburg for the suppers of the Czar's aristocracy. They are nice enough even in our days although now they smell of diesel oil at times; oysters and french fries with mayonnaise are still part of Ostend's peace-time distractions when the sea is too rough for bathing.

It was certainly rough just then, when Michael and his fellow soldiers were wading ashore from the Weasels, climbing the dunes, running back to the beach. It was already October and Europe was entering its sixth war winter.

Day after day a penetrating rain descended on them. The sea was wild. Half the houses in the little town were in ruins and Michael was one of the unlucky ones quartered in what was left of Ostend Casino. The Casino had no heat and canvas sheets propped up by wooden beams were supposed to keep out the steady gale blowing in from the North Sea. In a desk in a roofless salon Michael had found a box full of postcards of the place, in the sepia tints of prewar. They were curled and spotted but on them you saw gentlemen in moustaches and ladies in boas eagerly gathered around a roulette table. "Greetings from Ostend," it said on them.

Michael had taken a dozen and he was planning to send them to his friends in the States, the first chance he would get to mail them in Antwerp. Thinking up funny messages for them was right then his pleasantest occupation.

When the C.O. declared himself satisfied with the way his troop went about capturing the empty German pillboxes and bunkers in the dunes of Ostend, everyone expected to be shipped to a battle zone with great urgency, but nothing happened.

Wars have those hiatuses, and no one seems to know whether they are all part of a cunning plan or whether the crucial moving order has fallen behind the filing cabinet.

PERVERSELY, THE FIRST day of rest with no orders and no exercises was also the first day with no rain. A weak sun came out and the North Sea glittered as if it were the Mediterranean. Michael decided to go see how that landscape, etched in his mind as gray on gray, a landscape well-nigh made to get killed in, looked in sunlight.

He found out that now he could, in one go, run up the very steep slope he had done before on hands and knees. He clearly did better without people shouting at him, even if they shouted encouragement. Dawson, who kept a friend's eye on him, had said that he left it to Michael himself to decide if he was fit enough to be in on an amphibian operation. Michael had been uncertain about it but getting up that dune in one run was reassuring.

He walked along the ridge of the dunes, the sea on his left, and on his right bare fields and farms which mostly looked abandoned. Then of a sudden he stood in front of a chapel built of brick, sitting in a hollow in the sand. Gilded letters on the brick wall said, "Notre Dame des Dunes," Our Lady of the Dunes. It rattled him. There was something ominous about it, as of a monument already built for the Number Four Commando men who would presently lie dead in similar sand dunes along this forsaken coast, up north in Zeeland.

He tried the door of the chapel; it was open. He sat down on one of the benches and looked at the leaded windows, miraculously not broken. They had modern painting, simple surfaces in bright colors, on themes of saints and water. A storm-tossed ship accompanied by a whale, that was Jonah, and behind the altar Christ walking on the waters. You wish.

He thought of that mystical island they were supposed to go fight over. Is it my fate to find my ending in Zeeland? he thought. Zeeland, sea-land, he repeated the word, waiting for some kind of insight, but none came.

THE FOLLOWING DAY a twenty-four hour leave was announced, and a van was laid on for those who wanted to visit Antwerp. There was no great enthusiasm, the town was under V2 fire. But at noon, still under a vague sunshine, Michael was ensconced on the glassed-in veranda of the once five-star Grand Hotel of Antwerp, one of the undamaged buildings of the port. Only officers were sitting around there but Michael had never let that situation bother him. The waiter who came shuffling up was clearly not happy with a sergeant customer, but when Michael ordered an amontillado fino, he cheered up. "I will see if we still have that in stock, sir."

"Well, do the best you can," Michael answered in a phonily hearty voice. Why do I order something I don't even like, he wondered. But I can't give 'em the satisfaction of asking for Coca Cola, after all. Look at all these red-faced gentlemen with all their stars and stripes and tabs and ribbons, decorated with the spoils of battle, so to speak. But you must say for them they don't look nervous about living under the V1s and V2s the Germans are shooting at them. Think of the nice rooms they must have in this place, bathtubs that fill in two minutes with lovely hot water, telephones that work.

When he came into the hotel, he had seen that next to the reception a Navy communications unit had been set up. I'm going to make a phone call, he now thought. Too fine an occasion to pass up. Mary. Better late than never. Maybe she has reemerged from where ever they had put her. It would be soothing to hear her voice.

The waiter had produced the amontillado and waited to see Michael take a sip. Michael smiled his appreciation at the man and went to the communications desk. From gentleman-connoisseur to humble NCO-in-trouble. "I'm in an emergency," he told the woman at the switchboard.

"Oh yes?"

"I have to reach my sister who is a Wren. Last I knew she was in Warsash near Portsmouth. Do you think you could call WRNS personnel, and find out where she's posted?"

"And why is that an emergency?"

"I got bad news from home—about our mother."

"We can't do private calls. You may try a wire from the post office."

"Eh, well—I should have realized."

The woman looked at his face and smiled. "It's not really to your sister, is it?"

Michael was going to protest but then he started to laugh. "It's my girlfriend, but we had a fight and I can't make up for I don't know where she is. That's still an emergency, isn't it?"

"Oh well, sergeant, since all's quiet on the western front. Here, write down her name for me. Come back in a while."

He returned to his veranda table. The sun had come out in force now and his sherry was sparkling like a seventeenth century Dutch still life. I bet you they'll get her on the line for me. He felt pleased with himself and gave the waiter a ten-shilling note. Back at the communications desk, the woman he had talked to was gone, but another had a message for him. "Women's Royal Naval Service has no Marie de Jongh on their records." Fucking hell. And here I was sure I'd get to hear her voice. What on earth has happened to her. When people talk of the chance they have wasted, I know but too well what they mean. Damn, damn.

He wandered through the old town and went in search of a cinema. He found one, it was showing a 1934 American Tarzan. Heaven knows where they kept that one hidden for ten years. On the wall outside a torn poster was still visible for a German movie with an actress called Zarah Leander, who was shown lying on a couch, looking out at the public with the German equivalent of a come-hither look. Her legs had been torn off. That was for the previous program which had run only a week or so earlier, when the German army was still holding Antwerp.

Michael had no Belgian money but the cashier was content

with a shilling. When he stepped into the foyer, he had a shock; it looked in there like a replica of the Philadelphia movie house from his childhood—or maybe of all Depression years movie theaters the world over. Purple wallpaper with orange flames on it, or were they flowers? Brass wall lamps with metal shades like Paul Revere lanterns. Slightly sagging banquettes.

Movie theaters seem to provide the main emotions in my life now, he thought.

He sat through "Tarzan" twice without worrying about how to get back to Ostend in time. I don't need Ginger Rogers to start crying over my childhood. Tarzan will do it.

Back out on the dark boulevard he waved at a jeep going by in a westerly direction and got a lift. The driver was a Free French commando and he only grunted when Michael tried to start a conversation. They were almost out of town when they heard the air raid sirens go off for a flying bomb attack. "Fucking Germans," the driver said, but those were the only words he spoke on the journey.

The jeep was open and Michael was happy with the feel of the cold wind around his head. This has been a rudderless day, he thought.

Two more lifts got him to the Ostend Casino and when he undressed, he felt something solid in the inside pocket of his battle dress, and couldn't imagine what it was. The sepia postcards. Of course, and here he had forgotten to take them to the army post office in Antwerp. Never mind. Those messages hadn't turned out all that funny anyway.

MARIE, IN MAY AND JUNE 1944

42

MARIE WAS SITTING AT THE WINDOW OF A CAFÉ IN LILLE. Lille is an industrial town in the north of France, close to the Belgian border.

A late spring had left the straggly trees almost bare so far. A fine rain came down on the passers-by, all pale, all shabby, all hurrying. After four years of German occupation there was a sense of fear in the air, as penetrating as the cold raindrops.

Marie was wearing a blue and white nurse's uniform and she had good false papers in her Red Cross satchel and a supply of French money. So far, she had guided three convoys of escaped POWs and pilots who had bailed out. Two POWs had lost their nerve near the Spanish border and turned themselves in, and a Polish pilot, who had jumped out of his burning plane over Cologne and who was now dressed as a curate, had insisted on going it alone. But she had lost no one to the Germans and had never been arrested or even questioned. And now things had suddenly gone awry.

Her contact in Lille had been a woman who ran a tobacco shop, and when Marie had reported there at noon for her next job, she had been told, "We haven't got a single cigarette in the house, my husband is ill and hasn't been able to go after them," which meant, the line has been compromised, and do not come back. Marie found herself in a situation which, she had been assured, would not occur: she was left to her own devices in the heart of France, without instructions or contact.

There had been no one else in the tobacco shop and when she came out, the street lay empty under the rain; she had decided there was no need for her to run away from Lille. She had a room in a boarding house where she had stayed before and where they knew her as a traveling district nurse. Madame Odin, the landlady, was as unpolitical as it was possible to be at that time and her innocence was reflected in the terrible meals served. Clearly she had never cottoned on to the existence of a black market.

Marie held up her hand when the barman looked at her, and the waiter brought her another coffee. Coffee in a manner of speaking, but it was warm. Let me calmly examine the situation, she said to herself.

A man suddenly loomed up, standing over her. Her heart skipped a beat, she already heard in her mind the guttural "Documents, s'il vous plaît." However, what the man said was, "That's no coffee, my little one ('ma petite'), no one should drink that slop. Let me offer you a little rum. Virgile here still has rum for the faithful."

"Thank you, but no."

"Virgile, bring the lady a rum. And me too. Do you mind if I sit down for a moment?"

She was in a rage because this man had made her face a suppressed terror of the Gestapo. "Yes, I do mind!" she cried. "Will you please fuck off? Ask Virgile to direct you to the nearest brothel, why don't you. Go! Go away!"

Everyone stared at her and the man smiled rather stupidly and went back to the bar. Goddamn, she thought, I better get out of here, he'll think of something to get even. She put money on the table and hurried off. She looked over her shoulder, thank heaven, he's not coming after me. But I'm back in the rain.

She stood there for a moment, looking at the café window from the other side now. A yellowish curtain with dirty lace edges, a bowl of wax fruit, and propped up against it, a black on white sign, *Interdit aux Juifs*, forbidden for Jews, in pseudo-hebraic letters. He could have had me arrested and killed, if he'd known.

But I'd have had him too. She put her hand in her satchel and touched her pistol with the tops of her fingers. Even if I get stuck here in France it won't be as before. It will never again be as before.

She thought about her mother. As long as she had worked as a guide, she had resisted the idea of getting in touch with her. It was simply too tricky, even a postcard could have done her in: farmers on Walcheren didn't get postcards from France. But she had wondered if she couldn't get her out in a convoy. It was intolerable that she was at the mercy of some *Gefreiter* making his rounds. It could be another year, who knows, maybe two. The rumor was that the invasion had been postponed until 1945—

She reached her boarding house and went up to her room where she took off her wet shoes and white socks. She sat on the bed and tucked her feet in under the bedspread. It was very cold in there.

That doctor! she thought. Why didn't I think of him before. Girard Antoine. Le docteur Antoine. He's the man I'll go see, I can risk the train ride, all in one military zone, Lille to Paris. Dr. Antoine, she had been told, could be trusted.

This doctor had never been part of their set-up, but on several occasions he had taken care of their sick. He was a veteran of the First World War and he had lost a leg at Verdun. The Germans treated such men with a certain respect. She didn't really like him, there was something spooky about him, but surely that was not a professional consideration. He would send her on to someone else.

She told her landlady that she had to escort a patient to Paris and that she would be back in two days, and she took the early morning train to Paris. She got through the control without a hitch and arrived at the Gare du Nord in the early afternoon. From there she walked to the Villemin hospital, just a couple of blocks away. At Villemin they'd put her up if they had a free bed in the nurses' dormitory; they knew her there as the Dutch nurse working in Flanders.

Dr. Antoine still had a working telephone, but there was no answer. Finally, it was already ten in the evening, she got him.

"Marie," he said. Yes, of course he remembered her. No, she wasn't calling too late. "Always glad to hear from you. Are you well? Still, eh, active?"

What a stupid question. "I'm working up north as a district nurse. I have a health problem of sorts, may I come and see you?"

"Of course, Marie. Tomorrow is a very bad day. Day after tomorrow, at two, is that good for you? Can I reach you if I have to change it? You're in Valenciennes, and with no phone? Well, see you here day after tomorrow at two, then."

Marie, in May and June 1944

43

WHY DID HE ASK WHERE I WAS STAYING, MARIE ASKED herself for the tenth time. Well, never mind. If you can't trust a war invalid from Verdun— It's a nice day, let's think of that, Paris surely has a better climate than Lille. Let's get out, I'll walk to Dr. Antoine, a long haul but safer. You never know what kind of checks they cook up in the metro.

The night before she had washed her nurse's uniform in the sink. The hospital dormitory only had a cold water tap, and the uniform wasn't quite dry, but it couldn't be helped. She quickly left, taking her satchel with her possessions with her. That was one thing she had learned early on: don't ever leave anything personal behind, not even if you plan to be back in ten minutes.

She followed the big boulevard all the way to the river, and came to Place Chatelet to find that it was closed off, even for pedestrians, with German guards everywhere. She had planned to sit in one of the cafés there and do some quiet thinking, but these were now out of her reach. She cut down a side street and crossed the Seine on the Pont Neuf. There were still book stalls on the quay, but what they displayed were romances, old German magazines, and pictures torn out of art books. She stopped at one which had a stack of old novels, and looked for something to read in the dormitory that evening. Or on the train back to Lille, if it comes to that, she thought.

Pierre Benoit, "Koenigsmark," just the thing for a train packed to the gills and coming to a stop every ten minutes. Three francs. The "Voyage en Russie" by Dumas, a nice-looking book, but seventy-five francs. She put it back. "A valuable book, madame," the stall vendor said. "I don't get such stuff any more."

"I'm sure. But it is too expensive for me. I'll take the Benoit."

"One moment. I see you are a book lover. I have something very nice, and it's only twenty francs." He rummaged under the table and came up with a book in a hard, dark brown cover. He held it open for her at the title page. George Sand. "Péché de M. Antoine." My old heroine, she thought. "Yes, all right then," she said, smiling at the man, and counted out the money.

It was only noon, she had two hours now. She went to sit on a bench at the river with her book and brought out the slice of bread they had given her at the hospital kitchen for breakfast but which she had reserved for her lunch.

"The sin of Mr. Antoine." Strange. A bad omen for seeing doctor Antoine? No. Very unprofessional, superstitious, nonsense.

But then she looked at the opposite page. And read, in the very small print, "Imprimerie Michel Beauchamp Rue Bailleul 5-7 Paris."

That book, and with that title, had been printed by Michel Beauchamp, eighty years ago.

THAT SAME EVENING she was back in Lille where it was still or again raining. She walked past the tobacco shop which was closed and shuttered. Even the empty cigar boxes which had provided the only window decoration were gone. She didn't slow down, of course, but marched on to the boarding house where she was told that they had kept a plate of potatoes in the kitchen for her, and that someone had brought a parcel for her which was on the table in her room.

She ran upstairs and found that it contained a bottle of aspirin. A note said that they were happy to have found some aspirin for her and hoped it would alleviate her migraines. She emptied it out on the table and patiently broke all the tablets in two, but there was no hidden message. Still, it was a contact because she had never set foot in the pharmacy that sent it and she had no migraines. It cheered her up enormously.

She had sat on that bench at the Seine for a very long time, staring at "Imprimerie Michel Beauchamp." And then, coming to a decision, had marched straight back to the railroad station where she had managed to squeeze into the next train back to Lille.

And throughout that long ride which included an hour's stop in the middle of nowhere because of an air raid, she had worried about her decision: she had fluctuated between cursing herself as a superstitious gypsy and her belief in that name, Michel Beauchamp, their guardian angel. But through it all she had thought, it's bullshit and now I'm really stuck.

And now here was the bottle of aspirin. Like a light behind a distant window when you thought you were lost. She hadn't been abandoned then, of course not.

SHE WENT DOWNSTAIRS to heat up her potatoes and she asked if she could have a look at the children's school atlas. Yes, it was a straight line from Lille to Ghent in Belgium, and from Ghent to Zeeland-Flanders across the Dutch border, and then by ferry from Terneuzen to Walcheren, if the ferry was still running. She knew the name of the farmer on Walcheren who was sheltering her mother, Wouter Dieleman, five miles southwest of the town of Veere. The distances weren't really much; if there'd been no war she could have gotten there in a couple of hours. She shook her head at herself. If there were no war, why on earth would she have wanted to go to Veere.

I'm just checking this out for the hell of. But then, indeed, if there was a gap in the convoys, she might try using it to pick up her mother, get her out, too.

And then she felt so exhausted that she couldn't eat her potatoes (the children fought over them) but just crawled unwashed into bed.

Marie, in 1944

44

THE MORNING CAME AND, SURPRISE, WITH NO RAIN. THERE was no hot water and Marie shivered herself into a cold bath to get rid of the train grime. Then she went to the aspirin pharmacy.

"I've come to pay for the stuff you sent over yesterday," she said. "I'm Marie, the nurse."

"I'll ask my father," the girl behind the counter said.

The pharmacist came out and told her Doctor van Weyhe had asked him to find aspirin for her and that she could come to his consulting hour if they didn't do any good, every afternoon from two to three. He explained to her where the doctor's house was. "He's from French Flanders," he told her, "that's why the Dutch name."

Van Weyhe turned out to be small, old, fragile looking, but nonetheless giving an impression of great calm. On those expeditions of hers, Marie had always needed to be the strongest. Big, tough men, bomber pilots and artillery majors, took their orders from her and expected her to know at all times what to do. Now van Weyhe gave her the marvelous feeling that she was after all just a young girl and that she had come to the right person for some fatherly advice.

He asked her to wait until he had seen the last patient, and then he had tea brought in and they sat by his fireplace in which there was actually a fire burning. "I have a patient who is a lumberjack. He pays me in wood," he told her.

"I was on my way to see someone yesterday," Marie began, "not a friend, but—" She interrupted herself. "How did you know where I was staying?"

"We made a lot of mistakes in the past two or three years," Van Weyhe said, "but we're learning." He smiled at her and she smiled back. "It's been a long time since I felt almost too warm, instead of freezing," she said.

"Ah. A fire. Best thing for the nerves, better than any pills." He got up and put another log on. "Well, Marie, the less connections, the safer, of course. I know you didn't know about me but I was told to keep an eye on you, so to speak."

"Will you then be my new—"

"Your contact person? Heaven forbid. I'm just a medical person. What I can tell you is, come back in three weeks, and I will have some word for you. And I have some money for you right now, for you to sit this out quietly. That boarding house is an excellent place. And if you get bored, come for tea. And if you are nervous, come and we'll have a fire in the fireplace."

"Could you give me a letter, doctor, a letter sending me to Terneuzen in Zeeland to pick up a patient and bring her to the Lille hospital? Maybe Lille specializes in some particular treatment? Is that a sound idea?"

Van Weyhe thought about it. "You have some business in Zeeland, I gather. It sounds pretty safe to me. But let me make certain. Possibly I could find a real patient for you. Come back tomorrow during surgery hours. But now, relax and drink your tea. It's herb tea but we like it. My wife refuses to tell me where she picks it."

Marie laughed. "Tea, fires—it's so peaceful here."

Van Weyhe puckered his mouth which made him look, Marie thought, like Ratty (Mr. Toad's friend). He sighed. "Ostensibly, my dear. I'd wish it were."

Before leaving, Marie asked him, "If you are free to tell me—do we know who informed on us? Have there been arrests? Have people been killed?"

"I can't say," the doctor answered. "I simply do not know. Except for one informer, the more people are warned against him, the safer. Amazingly, he is not hiding. I regret to say, he is a colleague of mine, a Paris doctor. His name is Gerard Antoine. One wonders—are you all right, child?"

Marie was very pale.

"Yes, I'm all right," she said hastily.

Michel Beauchamp. And yet he must have been such a bitter man. His wife thinking he was dead, a son he never knew—his own death—how? Where? All alone? I must try to think very hard, with whatever strength I can muster, of that long dead and buried man. I must think of him with tenderness. That is what he must have lacked most, the tenderness of a fellow human being. An outlaw because he had printed some of our sad, pathetic, utopias. How reckless humanity is, reckless with others.

Why is tenderness so rare? Why have I never thought with tenderness of his grandson who put my life under a new flag? I know now, because he nursed me and hated it. But he stuck with it, didn't he, Marie? You weren't very generous, were you, and a bit too precious about your embarrassments. You could simply have loved him for it, simply, simply. Wartime love, but proper and fitting.

Marie, in 1944

45

Marie got the doctor's letter, a travel permit to travel to Terneuzen in Zeeland, to attend to a patient and bring him to the Lille hospital. "Is there such a patient?" she had asked the doctor. She wondered now if she might use this for her mother if there wasn't.

"Look, my dear. It has the stamp from the Lille police commissioner."

"Yes, I see."

"*Ergo,* the patient's existence is proven."

The letter got her to Terneuzen, where she was told, yes, there was still a ferry running to Flushing but once a day only, and she had missed it. She found a room for the night in the little hotel of the town where her letter made sure there'd be no problem with the police check on overnight visitors. Then she went out and bought herself a bicycle, with wooden tires, and so decrepit that the local police requisitioning all bicycles for Germany hadn't wanted it. And the following morning she was cycling along the road inside the dunes of Walcheren, with Veere as her destination.

The morale of the local people was very low. The Allied invasion, predicted for that spring, had not come about. And in the meantime, bunkers and gun emplacements which the

Germans and their forced labor were putting up all over the island were turning it into what seemed an impregnable fortress.

Marie was keeping a low profile—once she had left Terneuzen behind, the doctor's letter no longer covered her movements. She didn't enter into any conversations. She had managed to buy a loaf of bread in Terneuzen and had told the curious baker that she was a Belgian nurse come to take care of a very sick child, which apparently satisfied him. She looked so disheveled with her wrinkled uniform and dirty hair, not to mention her pathetic bicycle, that she blended in perfectly with the shabbiness of the times. It was tough going on the wooden tires and a saddle of petrified and cracked leather. Every now and again she had to get off and continue on foot for a while. But she felt at peace and even quite happy traveling along those wide flat polders. She liked the limitlessness of the land up to its very distant horizon where the blue of the water and of the sky fused. She felt she was traveling into this island like one of those early explorers entering an uncharted wilderness.

The wilderness here was a new, man-made one, at war with the civilization of which she was the secret envoy.

Her grade-school Dutch history romance of the Zeeland freebooters fighting the wicked King of Spain long, long, ago (in the year 1572) had come to life with newspaper actuality; if her mother would turn out to be afraid of moving, she would tell her, "Now we are those pirates."

She left her bicycle at the edge of the road and climbed up the highest dune in sight. Standing on its top, alone in the landscape, on the strip of yellow sand within a shell of sea and sky, she became dizzy. It felt as if she were sucked up into the air and she thought that would be a true liberation, to dissolve—she shook herself and muttered, "What's the matter with me is, I've had nothing to eat since yesterday but a chunk of bread full of straw."

She stayed up there a long time; when she came down the light had changed, there was already a hint of evening in the air, and, still almost hidden, the cold of the night.

She went on, going north. She was on the lee of the island, not facing the North Sea but inland, across a narrow estuary, and here were no bunkers, no German soldiers, nothing and no one. Far off she saw a church spire rise out of mist, breaking the flat severity of the island. That would be the church tower of Veere. She came to a road turning west, away from the dunes, and saw a man carrying a rake on his shoulder. He pointed out the way for her to get to the Dieleman farm. Soon her presence, a moving blue spot in the misty evening, would be noticed there and Dieleman, alerted, sent Marie's mother up to her cupboard in the attic and carried their radio (illegal now) out to the stable and covered it with straw.

When he could see it was a young girl on a bicycle approaching, he went outside and walked toward her, and then everyone could hear his shout, "It's all right! It's the daughter!"

There was a lot more shouting then, and hugging, sobs from Marie's mother, laughter, barking dogs. Dieleman and his wife exchanged worried looks as they thought Marie wanted to stay there too, and when she cried, "No, no, I've come to get my mom, I'm taking her to England!" there was still more excitement, and stupefied silence from Marie's mother.

But when they were sitting around the kitchen table to eat, only the children couldn't sit still and kept laughing and asking silly questions and staring at Marie. The grown-ups had gotten rather quiet now except for Dieleman himself who asked Marie, "So you've bicycled right through the German Westwall, have you now?" and when that raised a laugh, he repeated it a couple of times more through the evening.

When they were finished and started cleaning up, Marie slipped out into the orchard until there were trees screening the house from her sight; she looked out over the fields covered with a blanket of mist and up at the sky with its touches of fiery red and the first stars blinking at her. She thought how difficult it is for us, poor human beings, to match our realities with our exaltations and expectations.

The following day was the sixth of June of the year 1944. In the evening, a neighbor from Veere came by and told them that the Allied invasion had started. The Germans had declared a state of siege for Zeeland and the other coastal provinces, and a six-to-six curfew. Access bridges, and ferries, to Walcheren would from now on be open only to the German military and civilians with special permits. After all her scot-free travel, Marie had got stuck.

Michael, in November 1944

46

On the first of November, a day that may have set a record, even for that corner of the world, in cold, wind, rain, and general misery, Michael was standing on the harbor quay of the Zeeland town of Breskens. It was four in the morning. Number Four Commando was to be ferried across two miles of wild water to Flushing on the south coast of Walcheren island. Other Commandos, of Royal Marines, were to land near Westkapelle on the west coast. All this in the teeth of the Waffen SS with their thirty artillery batteries.

Those batteries were now placed on the dunes and on the dike of Westkapelle (where there aren't any dunes), because the rest of the island was covered with several feet of water, and had been for weeks. The R.A.F. had bombed gaps in the dike the month before, expecting to force a German evacuation, but it hadn't worked. The Germans had moved their batteries to high places and stayed with them. Of the unhappy farmers on the island, some had gotten away but others had hung on, surviving in the attics of their flooded farms, freezing their toes off, moving around in their rowboats and waiting for the English or the Americans or the Canadians to land and get rid of the Germans for them.

The planners of the Commando attack had divided the

Flushing waterfront in sections and each section had been given the name of a resort town on the south coast of England. This avoided confusion for those men who had been to grade school in England, but it didn't help Michael who at P.S. 38 in Philadelphia had not learned the names of English bathing resorts. He did not worry too much about this; as a fourteen-year-old he had read "War and Peace" and had known ever since that the best-laid schemes of officers and men mostly go awry. What mattered to him and all of them was, they knew this was not one of those vanity assaults, the vanity of statesmen and generals, that is. Antwerp needed Walcheren liberated.

The commandos had also listened to a lecture on "The Expedition of 1809," when a Lord William Stewart with ten frigates had set fire to Flushing as part of the war against Napoleon, and a British admiral had commanded forty thousand men occupying Walcheren, where most of them had died of "the ague" (probably malaria). It didn't seem too uplifting a model to Michael but presumably it was meant to give a sense of continuity to his mates, their following in the wake of a lord of the realm and a full admiral. Clearly, that continuity could also be seen as proof that there is little new under the sun and no end to mankind's trail of violence and follies.

All this went through Michael's head, but it had no bearing for him on the reality of the battle that just had to be gotten through; of course not.

They had a seasick crossing while over their heads the shells flew, fired by a Canadian battery in Breskens, and coming down—they hoped—on the defenses of Flushing. When they got near that coast, all they could see was a curtain of smoke: Flushing was burning again, just as it had in the year 1809. But gusts of wind flattened the smoke and now they could distinguish the silhouette of a windmill against the fires in the town. "Surprise, we're on course," the lookout shouted, for that windmill stood on the mole they were heading for. First sight of Walcheren a windmill: the Dutch tourist board couldn't have arranged it better. The boat hit the beach and on cue the Canadian guns stopped firing.

BATTLE DESCRIPTIONS are by the very nature of things not to be taken too seriously. They pretend to an overview which in actuality no one has had, and they depict a fantasy of method and order, cause and effect, which has little resemblance to the real happenstance of controlled chaos. Four army Commandos and three Royal Marine Commandos landed on Walcheren on November 1, 1944, and in the early afternoon or November 8 it was all over, and the access to Antwerp freed. That was the story of the battle.

Four Commando was lucky, they had the lowest casualty rate. Other Commandos had casualties of close to fifty percent. Mines killed many, they had been sown all over the island and the Germans had no maps of them, or if they had, they had been destroyed (this, of course, is illegal under the Geneva convention).

As for Michael, he had been under fire before, but not fire like this. It was as if the very air over the sea wall and the waterfront boulevard was ripped into shreds by shells and bullets; there was one continued twang, twang, twang, as of the screaming of banshees, banshees of copper and steel. He had never heard such an awesome and unnatural sound.

No one could stay alive in it for more than seconds, and the men proceeded from house to house through the walls, blowing openings in them with explosives. This had the cozy name of mouseholing.

The weather had been too vile for air support, but some of the SS bunkers were impervious to the arms they had, and they radioed an emergency call for R.A.F. Typhoons. Michael's moment came when he was asked to knock out an anti-aircraft post before the Typhoons got there, and he and a man of his platoon brought up a Piat from the beach, dragged it through a gap in the barbed wire, and set it up in a half-destroyed building. A Piat is a small anti-tank mortar, and the first mortar shell knocked out the anti-aircraft guns. Just as well that it did, for it also brought down the rest of the building on top of them.

Michael dug himself out in time to see the Typhoons come in low over the sea and fire their rockets at the bunkers. That operation, in his own mind, was the best thing he did in the war and perhaps worth all those years of waiting.

When night fell, Flushing was a liberated town and Four Commando held hundreds of German prisoners. The wind had become of gale force and they had a cold and hungry time with no new supplies coming in. They debated on how to feed the SS soldiers and indeed if they should be fed or if they could bloody well wait till they had been taken off the island: it was already known then that the Germans let their Russian prisoners starve to death. But Dawson would have none of that argument. "I don't give a damn about them being hungry or not," he said, "but I don't want to demean myself." He congratulated Michael on his direct hit. "Brilliant," he said (not a word he used easily), and he also told them that the building which had fallen down on their heads in the process had been the Flushing town cinema.

This pleased Michael no end. Movie houses were continuing to play a special role in life.

Presently Four Commando had to cross the island to reinforce the Royal Marines, a rough march of twelve miles which they did in three hours. It was an unhappy landscape they passed through, flooded fields on their right, and rows of knocked-out transport on their left, with wounded men waiting to be taken back and dead men waiting to be buried.

There were still woods in north Walcheren in those days and a report came in of German snipers hiding there. They marched to the town of Domburg where Michael saw his first Zeeland civilians, two families who had survived the bombs and the flooding in the attics of their farmhouses, now destroyed by fire; they were huddled in a church which had suffered little damage. Seven Troop settled in that same church.

They weren't needed any more against the snipers, but they were told to join a Marine Commando in an attack on the last German beach bunker, marked W19 on their maps. The worst part of the job was getting an assault boat there in what was now a full-fledged storm, and finding a spot on the beach firm enough to position a mortar on. But once W19 came under fire from two directions, it was over quickly. The steel door opened and two soldiers who had survived came out with their hands up. That was in the afternoon of November 8.

They disarmed their two prisoners and put them in the bow of the boat. They got aboard themselves but then, no one would have been able to say exactly why, they waited with shoving off and starting the engine.

They just sat there and listened. There wasn't a sound but the wind and the sea—a shattering silence, it seemed to them.

A seagull flew over their heads and its cry made them smile

at each other. “First bird I’ve seen or heard on this island,” one of them said.

“They’re coming out now. Their war is over.”

Michael, in 1944

47

THE TWO FARM FAMILIES WERE STILL IN THE CHURCH, waiting, but they were considerably more cheerful. They had been given blankets and they were having a meal of spam and coffee, which the commandos heated on a portable gasoline burner. Michael went over to talk to them. Several of them spoke English. "That's a sou'wester going up to nine on the scale," one of the farmers said, pointing upward where the wind was howling around the church tower. "Those poor devils."

"Which poor devils?" Michael asked.

"Serooskerke, sir. Flooded deep. Some people are still stuck there."

"In the attics," A woman said.

Michael decided to have a look outside but discovered he couldn't open the door against the wind, and he gave it up as a bad idea. It was already dark, and the men brought out their big flashlights. One of the farmers' children found a candle behind the altar and they lit that, too. "Bloody cozy here," their lieutenant said.

That lieutenant's name was David Marles, he was a Welshman. Michael had hardly ever spoken with him; Marles had been seconded to their headquarters. Now he seemed to make an effort to be friendly with Seven Troop. He told Michael how this church was not unlike the one his parents used to take him to, and how he had sung in the choir as a boy, and how— Michael had great trouble staying awake through it.

WHEN HE CRAWLED out of his sleeping bag at dawn and shuffled to the table where the coffee was waiting, Marles came up to him and said, "We took down a radio message from the C.O. Want to read it?"

First my coffee, Michael thought, but he answered, "Yes, certainly, sir."

The message was to all units and in it the C.O. told them that Walcheren was liberated and that a convoy would soon be on its way to Antwerp. The prime minister was sending his thanks to the commandos, to be passed on to every last man.

"How nice," Michael said. "We must think up a polite answer. How about, 'Our pleasure?'"

Marles gave him a dubious look. "The wind is dropping, we have a reasonable forecast," he said. "I'm told they are sending us two or three shallow-draft boats, for there are still natives on some farms or even on the roofs. I'll take one and I'd like you to run one."

"Okay, lieut," Michael answered and went to get his coffee.

Presently three naval ratings arrived in two boats. "At least we don't have to walk far," Michael said to the lieutenant. He hadn't realized the night before how close the water had come to the church. It was sitting there like a lonely lighthouse at the end of a narrow pier. They looked at their map to divide the search area, but it was not easy to translate the red and blue map markings onto the featureless, gray, plain of water facing them.

Marles shrugged. "Let's not worry too much about map

references, Beauchamp. You head east on the compass and run circles, and I'll run west. Take a Very pistol in case you get lost."

"Maybe I should take one of those locals along."

"Fine with me. A good idea. If there's one willing."

The man who had told Michael the evening before about the sou'wester was ready to come along. "Especially if you bring some cigarets with you, sir. My name is Pieter."

"Don't call me sir, Pete," Michael said.

They set off in the direction of the rising sun now weakly peering through the clouds. The wind had indeed dropped considerably but the water, even on the shallow fields, was still rough with unpleasant, short, waves which made the boat shake and vibrate. After a while they saw some farms sticking out over the water. "That was Vrouwenpolder," Pieter announced. "Small village."

They circled around it, Pieter shouted, "Hallo!" a couple of times but clearly no one was left there. A little house, barely sticking out over the water, vanished under the surface while they were looking at it. "It's a month now," Pieter said, "the flooding, I mean. It weakens them."

"Shall I push off?" the rating asked Michael.

He thought about it. "I guess so, don't you? We're to circle. What do you say, Pete?"

"Southeast, sir. Serooskerke, Gapinge."

"Southeast it is then. We should zig-zag a bit, large zigs and zags, I mean."

They moved on the arc of an ever-widening circle. Clouds chased across the sky and when the sun came out again, it threw a ring of rainbow colors. "Ring around the sun," Pieter announced. "More storm coming."

No sound was heard but the put-put of the outboard motor and the slaps of the waves hitting the boat. The rating, who didn't look older than sixteen to Michael, was sitting aft, steering and focusing on his cigarets which he was chain-smoking. Pieter, chain-smoking too and closing his eyes with pleasure at each puff, sat on a portside box containing a set of Very pistols (they're used to send up colored signal flares). Michael sat in the bow, staring out over the water.

I've seen this before he thought, a news photograph. No, it had color. A painting. An old Dutch painting of the World after the Deluge, in the Philadelphia Art Museum. Breughel or someone like that. How perfectly fitting. Except that our flood is man-made.

A gull flew high overhead, cried and dipped, coming straight at them, no olive branch in its beak though. It flew on, touched by a single beam of sunlight.

Is this how the whole world will look after the next, truly-last, war? This is sea-land all right, this Zeeland, the four elements, air, water, the earth, and the fire from the sun, but so mixed that you don't know where one begins and another one ends. This is how it all will really end, chaos, entropy as they taught me in Sheffield. You know what, Michael, he said to himself, this place is where I should go first when this is all over, build myself a cabin in the dunes, study the four elements and find wisdom. Horizontal, horizon, wisdom instead of the vertical one of those guys on the top of the Himalayas which rises and vanishes into the void. It would be a first all right, it would get me in the tabloids, the sea-level guru.

"When this is all over." He realized he had thought that so easily, no touching wood. No anxieties. I made it. No watery grave on Walcheren either. But that's not even it, I'm back in my skin, no Santa Lucia hang-ups, no Mary-and-Tom hang-ups. I got the whole world in my hand. Like in the song. He felt a sudden marvelous lightness.

"A roof, sergeant," the rating pointed and steered the boat toward it. But there was no sign of life there. The boat turned and resumed its previous course. It started to rain, and so heavily that most of the visibility was lost. The rating, and Pieter, seemed to concentrate now on keeping their cigarets dry.

It became a dreamlike procession to Michael, as if they were traversing a misty lake way below the surface of the earth, nature as distant and untouchable (and overwhelming) as in those gravures in the old Jules Verne books he had read as a child. "Journey to the Center of the Earth," he said aloud.

The rating stared at him. "Another roof, sergeant," he said sternly.

Yes, I better pull up my socks, Michael thought, no more fantasies. He cupped up some water and wetted his face. The water was very salty; God, he thought, it's like plowing with salt, the destruction of Carthage. Poor country.

The rating was circling the roof. Nothing. The rain let up some and they could see two or three other roofs in the distance, just red flecks in the gray. A dead dog floated by and then there was a thump, they all started. The boat had hit a dead cow floating just under the surface of the water. They looked at each other, and then back where the cow now had its feet sticking out. Pieter opened his mouth, he was going to make a joke but thought better of it, it seemed.

The rain persisted but behind them the sun was coming out and far off they saw light flicker, as of sunlight reflected in glass. The rating made for it without saying anything.

When they had come much closer they could see the red

light was indeed the reflection of sunlight in the cracked windowpanes just under the roof of a farmhouse. They glittered falsely as if the rooms behind them were on fire. "Hello!" they cried. Silence.

But as the boat turned off, Michael saw a light behind a window on a farm much farther off. He stared, it was different from the sun reflections. The sun went in and he could still see a point of light, and it moved, it moved to and fro behind the glass. We found someone.

"There!" he called out. The rating nodded, he had seen it too.

They put-putted toward the light, they seemed to go painfully slow of a sudden. But then all three at the same time could see a face behind the broken glass of the window. The water was high here, it almost reached the windowsill.

The rating steered the little boat right up to it. "Step back!" Michael shouted at the person behind it and he knocked out the remaining glass with his elbow. "Here, ma'am, put your foot here."

For it was a woman, wearing a variety of clothes on top of each other and holding an oil lamp which she now dropped in the water. They heard it sizzle. She looked at them and climbed out, tears running down her face. "We, we—" she stammered.

"Anyone else in there?" Michael asked.

"Yes, yes!" she cried but then she fainted on the bottom of the boat, and Pieter actually threw his cigarette away to have his hands free for helping her.

Michael climbed into the window and looked around. The water was some three or four feet high in the room, papers and debris were floating around. He waded toward the door and made the round of the rooms, calling out, but there was no response.

He came to a staircase, very steep as they are in Dutch houses. It had been wrenched apart by the force of the flood and there was a wide gap in the middle. As he stood there, he felt the house shift. He hesitated, he was becoming numb with cold from the water that came up to his middle. But then he heard a sound from the floor above, a weak "Here, here." He climbed up and found himself in a dark attic.

Its only light came from a tiny triangular window, but he could see movement, a human being, on a mattress in the corner. He carefully walked over, testing the planks before putting his feet down. A girl or a young woman was lying there under a pile of blankets. Two kitchen chairs had been used to raise them up over her legs.

"I broke my bloody leg," she said in English when she saw a man in a British army uniform come nearer. She was trying hard to keep her voice steady. "I can't get out of here."

"We'll help you, miss," Michael said cheerfully. "Don't you worry now." He kneeled beside the mattress and peered at her face in the half-light. And then a shock went through him as if he had touched an electric wire.

"Fucking hell," he muttered. Then louder, and in a blissful voice, "Holy Jesus. If it isn't our Dutch Wren. If it isn't our Mary."

•

• • •

SEEN FROM ABOVE, watching their movements on that small island from outer space, so to speak, their coming together like this wasn't all that astonishing. But seen from within the chaos of those days it appeared as extraordinary to them. A fated concurrence.

The war in Europe still had half a year to go; they'd survive.

But that moment in the attic of the drowning farmhouse was the best they would ever have together.